THE ESCAPE OF

GIANT

647

By
D.B Gilles

D. B Gilles

PPB

New York – London – Paris

Lauvern Press

A Division of PPB

}{

The Escape of Giant 647

Published by Lauvern Press

A division of PPB

Cover Design: King of Designer

Edited by: Carlo DeCarlo

Printed and manufactured in The United States of America Bookman Old Style font

ISBN: 9798786665902

FIRST EDITION

January 2022

Library of Congress Cataloguing-in-Publication Data has been applied for.

There were giants in the earth in those days, and also after that, when the sons of God came in unto the daughters of men, and they bore children to them, the same became mighty men, which were of old, men of renown.

GENESIS 6:4

PROLOGUE

1897

Adirondacks High Mountain Range
State of New York
United States of America

The ceremony was rushed and without fanfare. The twelve, burley farm workers the monks had recruited from the nearest town had never participated in anything like this. Despite their curiosity, none questioned the orders. All they knew was that they were there to dig a pit and put something in the ground.

They had endured a bumpy two-hour ride in a covered wagon. When they left, the temperature was bearable, but by the time they arrived, it had grown colder. Times were tough and there was money to be made. They did as they were told.

That they were blindfolded for the journey made no sense to them.

They got off the covered wagon and were immediately told to undo the blindfolds. As they did, Abbot Richard wondered if they were enough manpower. They were handed shovels and told to dig a hole twenty feet long, fifteen feet wide and six feet deep. Abbot Richard told them where. It took three hours.

They couldn't tell what was being buried because it had been wrapped in sheets and burlap. All they knew was that it was huge. They dragged and pushed whatever it was to the pit, then with great difficulty shoved it into the ground.

"That will be all," said Abbot Richard, his soft voice oddly soothing, to the workers. "You will be paid upon your return to your town. Go to the covered wagon and put on your blindfolds. Do not look back or there will be severe consequences. Do you understand me?"

Each of the dozen men nodded and did as he was instructed.

To himself, Abbot Richards thought, *Next time we must find a better way.*

This was the second giant to die. The first was buried by the monks and it was an ordeal. They were weak and out of shape, which is why he got the idea of going to the towns people.

He waited until the covered wagon disappeared, then waived the lantern light three times. Within seconds, twenty of the monks who lived at St. Alban's monastery appeared, in work clothes, ready to bury Jonathan.

"Let's be quick," said the Abbot. "It's late, it's cold and I'm very tired." The wind from the Adirondacks made it even colder.

"Shouldn't we say something, Abbot?" asked Brother Steven.

"No. He was trouble."

"He lived with us for a long time. Don't we owe him something?"

"We're lucky to be rid of him. He was difficult from the start. The ones who aren't trouble will get our blessing. Let's get to work."

Brother Steven nodded his agreement with reluctance. In the eleven years he had known Jonathan he'd grown fond of the cantankerous giant and felt that something should be said.

As the other monks shoveled dirt into the grave, Brother Steven paused for a few moments and said the following: "Dearest Jonathan, I bless you. May God have mercy on your soul."

He quietly prayed an Our Father, then resumed shoveling the dirt into the giant's grave.

Abbott Richard was more concerned with finding a more efficient way of burying the giants when they died. They had been put into the forest as children in 1886 and barricaded on strict orders from The Vatican. Now there were fifty-seven of them and nine of the females were pregnant. All of the women were of childbearing age. He knew that most giants didn't live past forty. He wondered how often they would have to bury them. There had to be a better way. It was risky bringing in the towns people, even those from two hours away. They would get suspicious.

Burying the giants had to be handled by the monks; otherwise there could be trouble. His immediate reaction was cremation, despite the fact that the Catholic Church forbade it. He would have to give the matter serious thought.

Three hundred yards away, hidden in the centuries old, towering trees which were part of the vast forest adjacent to the monastery, several pairs of eyes observed what transpired.

"Jonathan," his wife called out as she held back tears.

DAY

1

CHAPTER

1

Adirondacks High Mountain Range
Hammerhead Mountain
Cassoulet Nature Reserve
State of New York
United States of America

Seventeen-year-old Juliet Pine was one of three passengers on a Cessna Skyhawk flying to Plattsburg International Airport in northeastern New York, forty-eight miles from the Canadian border. She'd been drifting in and out of a sleepy haze caused by the two Advil's she took before the plane left LaGuardia Airport in New York City.

Two days before, during the flight to New York from Denver, her hometown, it was the same. She would toss and turn in her seat, not quite comfortable, fighting the first stage of the flu.

She was sleepy, but still able to participate in the conversation with her fellow passengers, Georgette and Luke, both recent high school graduates, like her, going to rebuild houses for a week with Habitat America. Georgette was from Alabama and Luke from California.

They were talking about Hammerhead Mountain, which they were approaching, and how it got its name.

"It was after World War One," said Georgette in a heavy southern accent.

"I checked it out on Google," said Juliet. "Planes were new and dangerous. A pilot delivering mail saw the mountain peak for the first time and he told other pilots that it looked like a hammerhead shark."

Georgette nodded her head. Luke made a face, as if to say 'hammerhead shark?'

"You know," said Juliet. "With a flattened head that extends outward and looks kinda like a hammer."

Luke thought for a few seconds. "Oh yeah. I saw one on Shark Week. Nasty."

"Nobody had ever climbed all the way to the top back then," said Georgette. "The view from the plane clarified that it looked exactly like a hammerhead shark, so that's how the mountain got its name."

"Why was he delivering mail?" asked Luke, his low-pitched voice sounding more like a professional announcer than a teenaged boy.

"Those were the early days of aviation," said Juliet. "Pilots who were in World War One tried to make a living flying in rickety planes. They were all young guys in their early twenties trying to make a life for themselves. Some were crop dusters, others delivered mail, a lot were daredevils and others were like Lindberg."

"They would crash all the time," said Georgette.

"Whose Lindberg?" asked Luke.

Juliet and Georgette glanced at each other.

"Duh!" said Georgette. "Charles Lindberg?"

"The first person to fly across the Atlantic!" said Juliet. "I mean..." She rolled her eyes.

"Oh yeah. Right. Charles Lindberg. The Lindberg baby. Somebody kidnapped his kid, right?"

"Yes."

Juliet had met the other teens through Twitter four days before the flight and didn't really know them, but they seemed nice enough. She was happy for the opportunity to talk and bond a little with them.

If only she could shake the flu, but Juliet was tough and wouldn't let a little flu get in the way of making new friends. Despite the fact that people considered her to be nerdy, she prided herself on having resolve. She was president of the debate club, vice-president of the chess team, first-string point guard on the girls' basketball team, sports editor of the high school newspaper and

trumpet player in the school band.

Maybe she wasn't exactly catnip to boys, but that didn't bother her. She didn't have time for silly distractions. Although she would have liked to have gone to prom with a date instead of her two best girlfriends.

College was the primary thing on her mind. That she would be going to school in Manhattan, the place she felt was the greatest city in the world, thrilled her. She was majoring in journalism at New York University in the fall. She couldn't wait for freshman orientation the last week in August and her first class the day after Labor Day.

The one thing bothering her was the argument she'd had with her sixteen-year-old brother, Greg, who accompanied her to New York. Originally, their father was supposed to come too, but he had to back out because of a water pipe that burst and flooded their entire house. He insisted that Juliet and Greg go and have a good time.

On the day their flight landed in New York, due to a freak accident on the tracks, the Air Train from JFK Airport into the city wasn't in service so they, and a thousand other travelers, had to wait for a taxi: three hours.

Their plan was to spend two days sightseeing in New York, then Juliet would fly upstate, work for a week at Habitat America then return to Manhattan. For the next five days they would finally enjoy the vacation they'd put off for nearly a year, after their mother passed away. Juliet was crushed that their father couldn't be with them. He really needed to get away. As an amateur painter, he had planned on visiting lots of art galleries and, especially The Metropolitan Museum of Art, with his kids.

Now, Greg, who wasn't into art all that much, would be able to spend a couple of days by himself exploring the city until Juliet got back. She wasn't worried about him. He was a loner. She knew he would find ways to entertain himself.

When they arrived at the hotel, a quaint boutique place in Greenwich Village, there was a mix-up in reservations. The hotel had them arriving the *next* day. The desk clerk gave them a tiny room, which Juliet hated. She was upset that her brother wimped out when it came to demanding an upgrade or at least something with a view better than the heating unit of the apartment building next door.

She loved her brother, but she understood that he wasn't the alpha dog in their family. Her mother was and Juliet took after her, so she tried to negotiate a better room and failed.

She spent the bulk of her time in Manhattan sick in bed. When she left the next morning, she gave her brother a curt goodbye, which she regretted almost immediately.

On the bus ride to LaGuardia Airport, Juliet decided to call Greg once she was settled at the construction site and make things right. She would be back in New York in seven days.

Seven days was nothing.

~~~~~~

A drizzle pattered against the small plane fifty-seven minutes after they took off, then eighty-five minutes into the flight, the rain came down suddenly and fiercely. Had Nick, the pilot, known about the storm, he wouldn't have even taken off. It literally came out of nowhere.

The plane shook violently and dipped. Juliet, Georgette and Luke all stared at each other, paralyzed and speechless. Then the plane went into a tailspin. All three were both screaming.

"Oh my God!"

"We're crashing!"

"What's happening?"

The heart attack had come on suddenly for the pilot. One minute he was fine, trying to maneuver the plane in the storm, then his left arm stiffened, his chest tightened and he lost control of the yoke. The Cessna sheered off course, making its way helter-skelter over the nature reserve, which was a no-flyover zone.

He couldn't breathe as the pain in his chest intensified. He knew he was having a heart attack or a stroke or maybe a cardiac arrest. The plane was going down and he did his best to guide it towards the clump of treetops that, from having flown in three other students the day before, he knew was The Cassoulet Nature Reserve adjacent to Hammerhead Mountain.

He shouted to his three passengers, breathlessly telling them to prepare for a crash landing, then he fell unconscious, his hands let go of the yoke, the plane sputtered and glided into the leafy tops of several ancient trees. It flipped over then slid halfway down a huge tree trunk where it came to a stop eighty feet from the ground, hanging precariously on heavy branches. After several seconds, the fuselage started to steady out, but then it slid down another ten feet.

Juliet was jostled from her seat, striking her head against the window and being knocked unconscious. She hung, partially upside down, entangled in her seat belt. She came to twenty minutes later, awakened by the simultaneous flash of light and roaring crack of thunder. The plane turned quiet, except for the patter of rain. She looked out the window and saw the side of Hammerhead Mountain.

Even though she was upside down, out of the corner of her eye she noticed Georgette and Luke. Both of their bodies were out of their seats and lying still, contorted, bloodied.

"Georgette?" she said softly. "Georgette, are you all right?"

No answer.

"Luke? Luke?"

She tried to maneuver herself to an upright position, but couldn't. She stared at her two traveling companions until the realization sunk in that they had stopped screaming.

She wondered if they were dead.

Then she passed out.

DAY

2

Eighteen Hours Later

CHAPTER

2

Juliet opened her eyes. She heard birds chirping. She looked out of the broken window next to her and noted that it was daylight. There was a slight misty rain. She wondered where she was.

The first thing she noticed was that her nose was unplugged. She felt better. She could actually breathe. She took three deep breaths.

My flu is gone.

But she was thirsty. So thirsty. And hungry. For some reason, visions of pancakes with blueberries smothered in maple syrup filled her head.

Wish I had some Gatorade or a bottle of Rocky Mountain water.

She loved Rocky Mountain bottled water because it was made in a plant three miles from her house.

If she craned her neck, she could see her wristwatch. 2:18

Then something dawned on her.

Why am I upside down?

She felt like one of those salamis hanging in a window in the delicatessen around the corner from her hotel. She was dizzy and an intense pain ran down the right side of her body. The top of her head ached. She raised her right hand to try and touch the bump on her head, but couldn't lift it, so she tried it with her left hand and felt something, a lump.

Because she'd been half asleep during the crash, she had no idea why they weren't in the air.

Her body was entangled in the seat belt, which had come partially undone and had saved her life. She tried to move, but because of the contorted position she was in, couldn't.

Suddenly she felt the plane slipping downward. It seemed to move fifteen or twenty feet before coming to a stop. She strained to lean forward and look out the window when she realized that the plane was in a tree. She tried to shake herself free, but couldn't muster enough energy.

She noticed the pilot hunched over in the cockpit. His neck appeared to be broken and what looked like a spike protruded from his chest, but because she was so drowsy Juliet didn't realize he was dead.

"Why aren't we in the air?" she mumbled softly.

Silence.

She couldn't remember the pilot's name for several seconds.

"Mister Pilot? Sir?"

Then it came to her.

"Nick?"

She saw Georgette and Luke. She remembered the grotesque expressions on their faces and their distorted bodies.

They're as old as me.

"Nick, what's happening?" she cried out.

She smelled something unlike anything she'd ever experienced. Sickening and almost sweet. She'd heard about the odd, disgusting smell.

It must be death.

She started screaming, "Help! Help! Somebody!" But no one came.

She tried to finagle herself out of the entwined position she was in, but had no luck because her right side hurt so much. By twisting her body a tad to the right, she could see out of the window. She saw nothing but trees, huge gigantic trees.

The plane crashed in the reserve. What was its name? Cassoulet?

She maneuvered the left side of her body and was having some luck reaching for the strap that had locked her in, when she saw something that immobilized her.

A huge brown, bloodshot eyeball with yellow spots, red dots and jagged veins in every direction stared at her through the broken window.

It blinked.

She recoiled.

It blinked again and she screamed, which caused the eye to blink again, more like a flutter, and move. Seconds later she saw human fingers – unimaginably large fingers -- trying to wriggle through the broken windows, coming toward her, twitching as they tried to avoid the glass shards.

They were dirty with chewed, grotesque, broken nails. The pinky was missing and scarred over. The skin was tough, scabby and filled with more scars, some new and some old.

She also heard grunting sounds, like noises of frustration. The grunting increased as the fingers wiggled through the broken windows.

Those are fingers.

Human fingers.

They're coming towards me!

One of them, the index finger nipped her foot, which freaked her out.

She screamed again.

What the hell?

Her scream triggered more agitated grunting and more finger twitching.

She tried to get away from them, but she was unable to move more than a few inches.

One brushed against her leg.

Please let me wake up from this nightmare!

For several seconds, she stared at the fingers incredulously, fear shaking her out of her grogginess.

They struck her as being roughly eighteen inches long. She was overwhelmed and convinced more than ever that she was dreaming. Her side and head were beginning to throb.

Then the plane began to tilt. It moved downward about three feet. The huge hands hung on to the open window and moved with the plane as it slid another five feet. Then another six feet. She felt nauseous and started to hyperventilate. She looked out the window and saw a hand pressed against the plane. Whatever it was unsettled her because it was shaking the plane back and forth.

Is that a giant?

I'm in the middle of a very weird dream. Or is this not a dream?

Is this really happening? It can't be.

She closed her eyes and tried to fall back asleep, but she was so stunned to be staring at a giant that she didn't even try to wrestle herself away.

She realized that the grunting noises she heard came from him.

He was doing something to the plane, trying to hold it steady or balance it. Or...

Is he trying to lift it?

Juliet guessed that he was at least fifteen feet in height, maybe more. She couldn't see much of his body, but she could see that he was fat.

There are no such things as giants.

Then she heard a distinctive male voice in the distance.

"Get away from the plane," it said authoritatively in a crisp British accent.

British?

The giant stopped what he was doing.

"Girl inside," he mumbled, although it sounded more like a growl. His voice was deep, gravelly, and he had a pronounced lisp. "Dead bodies too." There was a British lilt to his voice too.

"I'll take care of her," said the other voice. "Get out of here. This plane is going to fall. Go back to your part of the woods, Victor."

His name is Victor. How did he get the name Victor? And why does the other one sound like he's in a British rock band?

"Girl mine," he said. "I find her. She in my territory."

It's kind of a cockney accent.

"She landed in the neutral zone," said the articulate one. "Get out of here now!"

"This not neutral zone," he whined.

"You're confused, mate. It is. You know how you wander off sometimes."

Victor scratched his head, wondering if he indeed had wandered into the neutral zone. "We need a cook for the abnormals."

"So do we."

Abnormals?

"I find her. Not fair."

"Go home."

"No!"

"She's injured. She needs help."

"I help her."

"I'll get Trevor."

Who's Trevor? Is Trevor a doctor?

"I tell Martin. He be mad."

Who's Martin?

"Tell him whatever you want. This is the neutral zone."

The giant grumbled, slammed the plane with his right hand, stood and stared at the fuselage for several seconds and then ran off.

Juliet tried to look through the window to see who was talking. What she saw unsettled her.

It was another giant, but this one appeared to be in his teens. She was taken aback by his appearance. His long black hair fell to his shoulders and despite the fact of his enormous size, he was well-built and incredibly handsome.

He looks like a rock star.

A giant rock star. A giant British rock star!

What is this place?

She noticed that his body was in exact scaled proportion to an actual human being. He wore a shirt and pants that seemed to be made out of burlap and a leather vest and boots. He had a quiver filled with arrows slung over his left shoulder and a huge bow over his right. It looked like it was twelve feet wide. She could picture him on a stage riffing on a guitar.

She decided again that she was dreaming and closed her eyes. Nick, Georgette and Luc were alive, the plane hadn't crashed and she was still fast asleep in the back. She stopped thinking about the giant.

There are no such things as giants.

The thought ran through her mind over and over again, until the giant spoke to her.

CHAPTER

3

His words resonated within her. She knew he was real.

"You have to help me, luv," the giant said. She'd gone to London with the Debate Club the year before. She loved British accents. "I'm balancin' on a tree branch and I can't pull you out. My hands are too big. On the count of three I want you to slide yourself to the door. I'm going to open it. Can you do that? Yes?"

His voice is so cool he could do voice over commercials. What am I saying? This can't be real!

"Can you *do* that?" he said louder, some irritation in his voice.

She remembered reading stories as a child about giants: *Jack and the Beanstalk, David and Goliath, The Big Friendly Giant.* She loved the book, but didn't see the movie. She'd seen a film a few years ago called *Jack the Giant Slayer* in which the giants were all ugly and grotesque and they sounded like monsters. The giants were always so mean, gruff, ugly and dumb.

Frightened and shaking, she nodded yes and said, "I can't get out of the seat belt."

"Okay," he said. He peered into the plane through the window nearest Juliet. She was awestruck at how big his eye was. She decided that they were the color of the old actor her grandmother liked, Paul Newman: ice blue.

He has Paul Newman eyes.

He pointed his right index finger inside the plane and hooked it around the seat belt. Juliet noticed a gold ring with elaborate carvings on it. With one twitch, he loosened the belt. Juliet was free.

He adjusted himself and seemed to be grabbing onto the plane. "Ready, luv?"

She nodded yes.

Is this really happening?

He just called me love.

"On three. One, two... three."

Juliet did as she was told. With great difficulty she lifted herself up and began to drag herself toward the exit door. Her right leg felt numb at first, but as she made her way slowly to the door, inch-by-inch, she felt some relief.

My blood is circulating again.

The plane was teetering even more. She wondered how high up it was. She smelled smoke coming from behind her. The pain at the top of her head had now gravitated throughout to right above her left ear. Finally, she got to the door, which the giant jerked open.

A huge hand reached inside, wrapped its fingers around her waist and whisked her up into the air and onto his right shoulder. She was next to the bow draped around his shoulder and a quiver filled with arrows.

"Hold on to me collar," he said and she did. "I want to move you before the bloody plane goes down."

She liked the feel of the rain on her face. She opened her mouth and stuck out her tongue. The raindrops soothed her, moistening her dry lips and tongue.

She started to feel weak again. Being lifted out of the plane so fast made her head feel as if it were going to explode. She wondered if she'd suffered a concussion or something worse.

As he shinnied down the tree, she bumped up and down on his shoulder. She guessed it was about thirty feet from the ground. He climbed down it in five seconds. He took her to an oak tree about thirty feet away and set her down.

"Stay here."

He turned around, went to the tree and climbed back up. Then he started shaking and pulling at the plane. Juliet noticed that it was now on fire.

"There are people inside," she screamed.

"They're dead."

"I know, but... "

With one final shove from the giant the plane slid slowly down the tree. She heard noises, branches cracking, then steel scraping against bark, then it was moving fast, then slow again, did a nosedive into the ground and flipped over onto its back.

The giant climbed down the tree and ran to the plane, looked inside and saw flames. Using his hands, he gripped the piping hot fuselage and pushed and kicked it to a large ravine roughly forty yards away.

With one final shove the wreckage careened into the ravine and disappeared in the tall grass and shrubbery.

The velocity of the fuselage fanned the fire. Thick, black smoke erupted from the plane, making its way upwards through the trees towards the sky.

Juliet observed that the smoke seemed to bother the giant.

He climbed down into the ravine and approached the plane. Juliet got up and with difficulty made her way slowly to the edge of the ravine. There was a small explosion followed by two more small fires.

The first thing he did was throw dirt onto the flames, muffling them. He looked around and spotted a seven-foot hunk of tree bark with a pointy edge. He used it to start digging a hole. He dug quickly. It was fascinating for Juliet to watch.

He's so fast.

He stopped using the bark and started using his hands, quickly scooping up clumps of mud and dirt. Then he grabbed the bark and began digging again.

After twenty minutes he managed to dig a hole large enough to conceal the plane. He dragged and pulled it to the hole and pushed it in, then feverishly covered it. The black smoke stopped. There was no trace of the plane.

The giant had seen planes flying above the area over the years, usually when he had climbed a tree to scout his location. Trevor had told him it was a no-flyover zone, which is why so few planes flew over the forest. Trevor explained that when one did it was either lost or having engine trouble.

He stared at his work for several seconds. Satisfied, he turned away. Before he could see her, Juliet hurried back to where he had put her down.

The giant climbed out of the ravine only to be greeted by an impatient Juliet.

"Hey! What did you do?"

He ignored her.

"The airport people will need to investigate the crash," she said.

"There won't be an investigation," said the giant.

"The National Transportation Safety Board or whatever it's called will have to investigate."

"No."

"What do you mean no? And the other kids' families will want to bury them and there's the pilot. I don't think you should've done this. When the authorities come they're gonna make you dig that up."

"Authorities won't be comin'."

What is he talking about? Why wouldn't they come?

"I know you saved my life and I'm grateful, but you shouldn't have done that," she said.

"I did it for you."

"For me?"

"You'll understand later. You're confused."

"I am not confused," said Juliet. "And I don't want to wait until later. I want an explanation now. I mean, why did the plane crash?"

"I don't know."

"Do you think the pilot lost radio contact or maybe fell off the radar?"

"I don't know what that is."

"I don't either, not really, but I heard the dialogue in a movie once."

"We have to get out of here," said the giant.

"Where are we going?"

He picked her up as if she were a chew toy with one hand.

"Shouldn't you be calling the police or someone? I mean... "

He placed her on his shoulder and said, "Hold on tight."

She continued. "But... but... there are rules that have to be followed after a plane crash. I know that because my aunt used to date a guy who worked for an insurance company that investigated plane crashes."

"It's hard to get used to being carried," he said. "We have a way to go."

Juliet got the feeling that the giant wasn't listening to a word she said.

"Wait a second!" she pleaded.

"Don't talk."

"Will you at least tell me what kind of place this is and who that other giant was?"

"No more talking!" he said, irritated, and took off. "Blimey!"

CHAPTER

4

Why is he running?

As she clung to the giant's shirt collar, Juliet was amazed at how fast he moved, weaving through trees along a winding path that went upward, then downward, then straight. It was covered with leaves of all shapes, sizes and colors, stones and sand, fallen branches, large and small boulders, hilly patches, tree bark, undergrowth and foliage of all kinds intertwined with smaller paths. It reminded her of a huge, unkempt garden.

She felt like a rag doll, bumping up and down. It was like riding a thoroughbred racehorse, which she'd done last summer, but better, and faster. She was five feet four and weighed one hundred and ten pounds. He carried her as if she weighed nothing.

As they moved briskly through the forest, she tried to check out where she was, but all she could focus on were trees of many different sizes and shapes intermingled with no set pattern. There were scores of them, hundreds, maybe thousands.

As she got her bearings, her senses sharpened. She noticed that the giant had a smell about him that she'd never experienced.

He smells like nature.

"Where are we going?" she asked.

"To where I live."

"Shouldn't the airport be contacted? Or paramedics? Or the Fire Department? Or somebody? Maybe they could've been saved."

"I wish you would stop talking and just rest. Your head wound could be serious."

Maybe he's right. My side hurts and I have such a headache. But I can move all right. I think I'm okay. Could I have had a concussion? No. I'm a little sore. Yeah. I'm okay.

"All right."

She stayed silent for roughly fifteen seconds.

"Where are we?"

"Don't talk."

"I just survived a plane crash. Don't you think I have a right to talk? To ask questions?"

"You're in a nature reserve next to Hammerhead Mountain," he said. "Its name is Cassoulet Reserve. No one is allowed in here. You're lucky to be alive. Planes can't fly over us."

"Then why was the pilot flying over it?"

"I don't know, but every five or ten years, pilots of small planes make a mistake or there's bad weather or they get cocky. The privately owned planes are the ones that usually come down. If the pilot is unlucky everybody dies. That's what happens most of the time. You were lucky I got there when I did, otherwise you would've burned to death. You'll have plenty of time to ask questions later."

What does he mean "plenty of time?"

"I have questions now."

"Please stop talking." He rolled his eyes.

"I need to call my brother and tell him I'm okay. And I want to get out of here."

"We have no telephones here."

What?

"How do people communicate?"

"We don't."

"What do you mean you don't communicate?"

"Not like you do."

"What does that mean?"

"We're isolated."

"I can see that. What kind of place is this?"

"I just told you."

"I know, but I need more information."

He decided to ignore her. He wondered if she was the kind of girl that Trevor told him about, the kind who never stopped talking.

But she's so pretty. Even after a plane crash, she's so pretty.

"My brother will be worried about me," she said.

He ignored her.

"I need to get in touch with him. He's in New York at our hotel. I was supposed to call him when we landed. He'll be worried sick."

"You can't call or see your brother. Ever again."

A hot chill ran down her spine. She began to shake. She felt tears form in her eyes.

Ever again?

"But... ? Why not?"

"Please stop talking."

I can't see Greg ever again?

CHAPTER

5

"That I can't see my brother again is crazy!"

"All your inquiries will be answered," he said.

"You keep saying that."

The giant picked up the pace and shut Juliet out.

"I won't be answerin' anymore of your questions for now."

"But... "

She felt herself slipping and losing her grip. She finally decided to keep quiet – for now -- and just try to hold on to him.

She clutched his collar with both hands, her left cheek pressed against his shirt, her right eye trying to take in where she was.

"Why are you running? It's hard to hold on."

"I have to get back to my territory."

"What territory?"

He ignored her.

As she clung to him, she took in her surroundings again. Besides the endless trees, there was a large stream or was it a river? In the distance, if she squinted her eyes, she was certain she saw a huge waterfall. She thought she saw a deer. Or was it a moose?

It was quiet, except for the rustle of the breeze. She had never experienced anything like it. There were no ambient sounds. No cars. No voices. No hustle and bustle. Just dead silence.

She wondered how it would be at night. In a forest with no lights other than what came from the moon. And how much moonlight would filter down through the denseness of the trees.

It would be pitch black.

Even though she was seventeen, she was still a little afraid of the dark. She always had a night-light on in her room. She wondered where she would sleep.

She speculated that if there were wild animals, loose, dangerous animals, it would be treacherous to be outside. She was terrified.

Then she saw a normal-sized woman with long gray hair standing next to a tree carrying a basket. She wore a brown dress that went down to her knees. She looked as if she were in her late sixties, maybe even older. She stared at Juliet as if she'd seen a ghost.

As they passed by the woman, Juliet looked at her, happy to see a normal-sized person, but wondering what she was doing here. Then she saw another woman with white hair down to her shoulders step out from behind a tree, who looked even older, than the first. Both of them stared at Juliet.

"Who are those women?"

"Gretchen and Margo. You'll meet them later. You'll meet everyone later."

Everyone?

"Who's everyone?"

"People like you."

"How like me?"

"Abnormal sized."

This guy's like a million feet tall and I'm the one whose size is abnormal?

"There are nine people living in my territory. Trevor and I take care of them."

Why does he take care of them?

And who's Trevor?

In the distance, tucked under an overhang between a cluster of even thicker trees and the side of a mountain extending several hundred feet upwards, Juliet saw the entrance to a cave.

The giant slowed down and stopped, reached for Juliet, gently grabbed her and set her on the ground. He put his hands on his knees and breathed deeply as he caught his breath.

She noticed that he was sweating, that perspiration was dripping off of him

"Let's go in," he said. "You need to lie down and eat something. Go ahead, luv."

She moved tentatively. She walked through a thick, roughly hewn wooden door about twenty feet high. The giant opened it and brought her inside.

"Uncle Pete," he called out.

She looked around and was amazed by the size of the furniture. There were chairs, something that resembled a couch, tables and they were all made of wood, built to scale for giants. They looked like huge versions of Shaker furniture. The room was lit by several two-foot-high lanterns with low flames, but as she checked out the rest of the place she still knew she was in a cave. She wondered *if* she *could* sleep in a place like this. And where would she go to the bathroom. She doubted this cave had indoor plumbing.

From an entrance that seemed to be part of a different cave, another giant lumbered in. He looked much older than Damian. He had a scraggly beard and long willowy white hair. He was fat, moved slowly and had a bad limp. His complexion was pale. He looked sickly. He wore essentially the same outfit as the younger one.

This one's name is Pete. I wonder what the one who saved me is called.

"There's been a plane crash," the giant said. "By Jawbone ravine. The pilot and two passengers are dead, but this bird's alive. She needs to rest. I'll put her in my mother's room."

Expressionless and unemotionally, the older giant opened the door to another room and within seconds Juliet was lying on an enormous ed. It felt like twenty king size beds all put together.

"Why did you bring her here?" Pete snarled, like the other two giants, in a British accent. He sounded like the Beatles. Unlike the young one, his voice was high-pitched and came out in a soft monotone.

"Victor found her first. He wanted to take her. I couldn't let him do that."

Take me?

Take me where? Oh my God! Will they be using me for sex? Is this Trevor guy a sex trafficker?

Two girls from Juliet's high school had been kidnapped last year and held in a sex ring. Juliet knew one of them. She and all her girlfriends were terrified it would happen to them.

"Why not?" said Pete. "They need her more than we do."

"We can save her."

Save me from what?

"Save her?" Pete smirked and shook his head. "Why would you want to save her for this? You should have let her die, Damian."

So, his name is Damian.

I wonder if he has a last name.

Why would the old one not consider rescuing me?

And why would he want me to die?

"Just hope her injuries aren't so severe that she'll need medical attention," said Pete. "If the monks find out about her, you know what will happen."

What will happen?

What the hell?

And who are these monks he's talking about?

"I'll tell Trevor. He'll decide the extent of her injuries. He'll know what to do."

Trevor again. Who is he?

"She could be a companion for him," said Pete.

Companion?

"Possibly."

What are they talking about, companion?

"She might be too young."

"She's a female."

"He'll want more than a companion."

What?

That comment jarred her even more. She sat up, but immediately felt dizzy and fell back down.

"As I think about it, Trevor's too old for her," said Pete. "This girl is still a teenager. She's probably your age"

"He'll want a mate."

A mate?

"A wife."

Oh my God! Please don't let this be some kind of sex ring thing?

"What he wants won't matter," grunted Pete. "Look at her. She's young and strong. She won't want to stay. She'll be like the other two from the breach four years ago. I can tell by looking at her. This girl is a runner."

What are they talking about?

What breach?

What's a runner?

And what other two?

And what's this wife crap?

"She'll make a run for it and then she'll die like all the others."

Die?

"For her sake, I hope not," said Damian. "I'm worried about Victor. He might try to take her."

Take me?

Pete looked alarmed. "They need someone more than we do. They have more people to take care of."

"I know, but... "

"Let them have her," said Pete.

"Trevor needs her too."

"It's not our decision."

"Trevor needs a companion."

"Let her decide on that," said Pete. "And since when are you looking out for Trevor? I thought you two weren't talking anymore."

"We aren't, but he's still my friend."

"You better make sure. After me, he's all you've got. Martin used to be *my* friend. Now look at us. We say nothing to each other."

Who is this Martin?

"I still talk to Trevor."

"Not like you used to. What you two had is gone." Pete turned his back to Juliet. "Enough of this nonsense. I'm concerned about you and me. Whenever someone new arrives they put us in jeopardy."

Damian lessened his attitude. Pete moved next to Damian and said, "We lost your mum the last time when the mountain climbers came."

"I know that."

He moved closer to Damian. "I don't want to lose you. If Trevor says she can heal without care, we'll deal with her. If she needs a hospital, we'll let nature take its course. What about the wreckage?"

"I buried it."

"Good. What the monks don't know won't hurt them. Or us."

Damian nodded in agreement. "I'll go now and get Trevor. Make sure she rests."

"Let me go," said Pete. "I need to walk. My back is acting up again and my knee aches. Moving helps." He glanced at Juliet, then said, "Where did you say the plane went down? I want to see how good you buried it."

Damian sighed and rolled his eyes. "You mean you want to make sure I did it right. It's in the south side of the ravine, past the stream. Buried near the x-shaped tree. You'll probably smell the burning oil."

"That isn't even our section," said Pete, irritated. "What were you doing there?"

"Hunting. I was havin' a bad day in ours."

"We're not supposed to be there and they're not supposed to be here. We get along fine when everybody obeys the rules." He shook his head back and forth. "So, Victor was right. You were in their territory."

"I was comin' back to ours when I heard the plane going down. I went to check it out. Victor was looking inside and shaking the plane. He would have knocked it to the ground and... "

"I don't want to hear about it," Pete grunted. He looked at Juliet and shook his head back and forth. "Bring her water and some fruit."

"Would you get some fresh clothes from Trevor for her to wear, Uncle Pete?"

Pete nodded, then limped slowly out of the cave. Damian calculated that it would take him an hour to pick up Trevor and get to the crash site and another hour to get back.

Damian looked at Juliet and stared at her face. He crouched down to get a better look. He couldn't take his eyes off her.

He had never seen a girl his own age before. He hadn't seen a female in five years, when he was twelve, and the one he saw was a skinny, unattractive mountain climber in her forties with bad skin.

Looking at Juliet was overwhelming. Because of the plane crash she looked ragged and bloody, but she was beautiful.

Blonde hair, hazel eyes, soft skin. Just like Trevor described the girls he'd known before he came here. Damian wanted to touch her. He felt a peculiar longing in his body that he'd never felt before.

He thought about romance and the romantic feelings Trevor told him about.

He called it love.

Love.

I wonder if I'll ever experience love.

"You love a girl and she loves you back, if you're lucky," Trevor told him. "If you're not she'll dump you and find somebody else. Or you'll dump her and you'll keep looking."

"Did you ever love a girl?" Damian had asked Trevor.

"I thought I did, but in hindsight it was more like puppy love."

"What's puppy love?"

"A teenage thing. It's a shallow romantic attachment."

The sensation in Damian's loins confused him, but he was certain it had to do with sex. Trevor had told him all about sex. The concept of it excited and depressed him because there were no female giants his age, which meant he could never have sex.

"Unless some day you can find a female giant," Trevor had told him.

Damian knew that because of the difference in their sizes nothing could happen between him and this girl, but he was grateful for the opportunity to see, up close, what a young girl looked like.

She's so pretty.

Maybe even beautiful.

CHAPTER

6

Hammerhead Mountain was located in Keene County. It's Chief of Police, Daniel Parterro, was having a bad day. He'd received phone calls from family members wanting to know the whereabouts of three interns working on The Habitat Project and the pilot of a missing Cessna.

The most insistent was a guy named Greg Pine demanding to know what had happened to his sister, Juliet.

"Mister Pine, I'm only the Chief of Police," he told him. He had no idea he was talking to a sixteen-year-old boy because Greg's voice was quite deep. "Plane crashes aren't in my jurisdiction."

"If it crashed, it happened in your jurisdiction," said Greg, trying to remain calm. "Can't you go look in this place called Cassoulet Preserve or Reserve or something?"

"No. I can't. It's government property. We'll have to wait until the National Safety Review Board gets involved."

"But... "

Parterro felt the guy's pain, but he could do nothing.

"All I can tell you is to wait for an official announcement that the plane has crashed. I feel your frustration, but my hands are tied right now. Until that announcement comes, there's nothing I or you or anyone can do. I'm sorry. I have to go."

"Alright. But will you call me as soon as you hear anything?"

"Yes sir. *If* I hear anything."

Parterro hung up. As he was musing about whether or not a plane had crashed, his phone rang. It was from James Monter of the National Safety Review Board inquiring about a crashed plane.

"Their flight plan had them flying close to the nature reserve adjacent to Hammerhead Mountain when all communication stopped," he said. "Have you seen or heard anything?"

"Not a thing," said Parterro. "To my knowledge no one else has either. I received no phone calls."

"Air traffic control lost all radio contact," said Monter. "I was informed that the reserve is nearly forty thousand acres. That's a tremendous amount of space. I understand that it's government property. If it's necessary, can we get in there to search without miles of red tape?"

"Frankly, if a plane went down the monks would know about it and I haven't heard a thing."

"What monks?"

"There's a monastery run by the Trappists up here. Besides them, there are always people making retreats. Plus, they have a small plant that produces jellies and jams. Someone would've heard a plane go down." He saw this as his opportunity to get out of the conversation. "Maybe you should call the monastery, but if the plane did indeed go down in the reserve it would've been yesterday. They would have contacted me or the airport or someone by now."

"You're right." Monter sighed deeply.

"I'll give you the number of the abbot. I hear they keep pretty good control over there. If the plane went down, he would know."

"Okay."

He gave James Monter the abbot's phone number.

"In the event you hear anything, please call me immediately," said Monter. "And don't give out any information."

"Of course not. Goodbye."

The last call came from Nat Harper of The Habitat Project.

"Not a word for thirty-six hours," Harper said. "I just heard that they think the plane might have gone down in the nature reserve."

"Mister Harper, that is a rumor," said the chief. "There have been no reports, no sightings, no nothing. I can't just put out a bunch of my men and have them start looking for something that might not be there. The reserve is thirty-seven thousand acres of dense forest."

"Then what happened to them? Tell me that. There's no ocean or lake or body of water where they could've ditched."

"Sir..."

"I've got their families on my back. One girl's brother keeps pestering me, not that I blame him. He wants answers. I need something. Even if they're all dead, you have to give me something, please!"

"I'll see what I can do," Daniel said, then hung up, feeling flustered.

Now he would have to call St. Alban's Monastery and speak with the abbot.

He remembered the first time he'd spoken with the man. He had only been on the job for three months. The Abbot was anything but soft-spoken. His voice was authoritarian and Parterro felt that the man was used to being in charge and getting his way.

A child had wandered off from a family who'd been camping near the monastery. It was the first time he'd encountered anyone from the monastery. He'd spoken with Abbot Gassner who explained that the Order had been granted permanent ownership of the nature preserve provided they treated it as such. Part of their arrangement with the government was that they would take care of the land, trimming the trees, planting, replanting.

The monks agreed and had done a fine job.

He'd asked if a young child had wandered off onto the monastery land. Could it be seen or could it be found?

"If a child wandered away in the daytime, we might have seen something," said the abbot. "But if it were at night, I think not. We retire here quite early. And our guests making retreats aren't permitted in the reserve, so there would be no one around to see him. If you like, I can have some of the brothers begin a search party, but remember, Cassoulet Reserve is a vast area."

"Anything you could do would be appreciated, Abbot Gassner."

"Of course. Good-bye, Captain Parterro."

The Chief of Police had gotten an uneasy feeling talking with the abbot, as if he were hiding something, but he could do nothing.

The St. Albans's monastery was a powerful force in the region, providing much needed employment through their Smiling Monk manufacturing company. He did not want to ruffle their feathers.

As luck would have it, the child had been found and there was no need for further communication, other than a polite call to the abbot with the good news.

Captain Parterro decided to let the airline people handle the conversation with Abbot Gassner if – or when -- they learned there was a crash. He disliked the abbot and everything connected to St. Alban's monastery. He didn't even like their jams and jellies because they were too sugary. He had heard the rumors and old wives' tales about the reserve being a place where monsters lived: Bigfoot, dinosaurs, giants, werewolves and a slew of other creatures.

He never believed any of it. He was from a long line of cynics and straight-shooters. To him, Cassoulet Reserve was exactly what it was presented as, a nature reserve filled with millions of trees.

He wanted this over with fast.

He dialed the abbot's number.

"Abbot Gassner," said the low-pitched, unusually serious voice. "May I help you?"

"This is Chief Parterro. We think a small, single-engine plane may have crashed in the reserve. I'm calling to find out if you know anything about it."

"Definitely not," Gassner said, sitting up. The last thing he wanted was anyone official wandering in the reserve. He set his Punch Gran Puro Santa Rita cigar in the ashtray in front of him.

"The National Safety Review Board just contacted me," said Parterro. "I'm calling you because they may want to come by with a search party if they have proof that a plane crashed."

"I personally think it would be a waste of their time," he said officiously. "It will be like looking for a needle in a haystack, assuming of course a plane crashed. We have a large retreat in progress plus our manufacturing plant is in full operation. With all our monks and workers, I can assure you no one heard or saw anything. I most certainly would have been informed if they had. Is this search party prepared to comb through thirty-seven thousand acres?"

"I don't know how they operate, Abbot, only that they're very thorough."

"That's good to know, but as I've said, if there were a crash, someone at the Monastery or our jelly production facility would have most certainly heard or seen it."

"I agree," said Parterro.

"We have nothing to hide, and our door is always open. If necessary, have them contact me directly and I'll tell them personally that we haven't heard a peep."

"Alright."

"Thank you for your call. Goodbye, Captain Parterro."

As he hung up on the Police Chief, Abbot Gassner went into instant defense mode.

The giants lived in the eastern section of the reserve, the farthest area away from the only entrance in the northern section. He knew that the first stage of a search by the airline people would be by helicopter. If they saw a trace of a plane, they would want to go into the reserve and perform a ground search. If they saw nothing, that would be it. He hoped that if a plane went down, it didn't happen in the eastern section, otherwise it would mean trouble.

It meant people would be coming into the reserve and they would be in the giant section.

Damn these pilots who fly near the reserve. Serves them right if they did crash.

He reached for his cigar and took a puff, then blew out the smoke in a series of rings.

Meanwhile, Parterro was content to presume that the plane might have crashed, but because there had been no phone calls from anyone who had seen or heard the plane go down, that it did not.

He just wanted it to be over. The Abbot gave him the creeps.

CHAPTER

7

Trevor Bruckner lived alone in a cave half a mile away from Damian and Pete. The nine other normal-sized people lived communally in a larger cave inside of Hammerhead Mountain, six women, three men. They were all older, in their late sixties and seventies, and one male in his fifties. Pete decided to pick up Trevor before checking the Cessna's burial site rather than going by himself. He wanted Trevor's opinion.

When Trevor first came to the giants twelve years earlier, he was a troubled, overweight, slightly odd nineteen-year-old boy who barely made it through high school. His high D, low C average was not indicative of his true intelligence. He was smart, but lazy, preferring to get stoned and break into people's houses instead of getting a job.

After the first two years with the giants, to keep from going crazy and out of boredom, Trevor decided to educate himself. Television and the Internet were out of the question, as were movies, radio and podcasts.

He loved listening to podcasts.

But all he had at his disposal were books. Because Trevor was young, the monks used him as a go-between with the giants. When the monks wanted to find out if a giant died or if one was sick, Trevor reported it to them. In exchange, when Trevor needed clothing or medicine or something to read, they reciprocated.

The monks had a voluminous collection of books, which Trevor requested and read -- philosophy, sociology, religion, psychology, the arts and the great literature of the ages, all the humanities. Because he arrived when Damian was five, despite their age difference, he soon became Damian's big brother and friend. He was shocked to find out that Damian spoke the King's English, as did his mother, father and every other giant in varying degrees.

That happened because their ancestors had been taught by a British mountain climber named Nigel Folquist, who was the first person to be held captive in the reserve in 1887. A linguist by profession, he willingly taught every giant who wanted to learn. They, in turn, taught their children and so on.

Trevor read every book the monks gave him, no matter the topic, to pass the time. He shared all the content with Damian. Whatever Trevor learned, Damian learned. He introduced the little boy to the world. Initially, Trevor felt it was a good thing, but as the years passed Damian had more and more questions about what he called "out there." By the time he was fifteen their relationship became strained largely because Damian had become obsessed with escaping.

Trevor tried to quell that line of thinking in numerous conversations.

"You're fifteen feet tall. If you ever got away, you would be captured and turned into a freak show. The Catholic Church has done you a favor by letting you live here. Stay put."

Damien obeyed him, but inside he continued to seethe. This was because of the oral history his mother told him about a race of giants living in the south of France in a forest near Mont Blanc.

And there was also the ring.

His mother had given it to him with great reverence, almost ritually. He wore it on his right index finger. He cherished it because his mother told him that it had been passed on through the centuries and that his family was descended from a band of warriors.

"You are a gentle soul," she said. "You are not a warrior, but you are a leader, Damian. This has been passed down from fourteen generations of your ancestors. Unbelievably, it came along with one of the children who was part of the child giants' migration to America. Perhaps you will have the opportunity to lead someday."

"Where?"

"Not here. In the mountains of Mont Blanc. If you can get there, then you will shine my darling."

"How will I get to France?"

"I don't know, my sweet boy. I don't know."

She gave him the ring when he was thirteen. Getting out of Cassoulet Reserve and to Mont Blanc was all he thought about since receiving the gift.

He argued constantly about Mont Blanc with Trevor.

"That is a myth," Trevor said repeatedly. "Your mother told me her oral history too. It's a very nice story, Damian, but it's a centuries-old tale. The child giants were all brought *here*. This was, and is, the last stronghold of the giants. The pope wanted them out of Europe, plain and simple. That giants once lived was to be erased from history. And it was."

"My mum wouldn't lie."

"I'm not saying she did. I'm saying that the story she told us had been repeated so many times before she heard it that it's difficult to believe."

"If I escaped, I could tell the truth about giants and what the Catholic Church did to us," said Damian.

"First of all, you would never get the chance because no one would believe you. Once the scientists and the government got at you, you wouldn't have one day of peace. Not one. Stop thinking about escaping. It will never happen!"

What Trevor never told Damian was that he didn't want him to leave. Damian was all he had. And as far as escaping himself, it was something he wouldn't allow himself to consider.

He knew that if Damian could somehow find a way out, he would want Trevor to come with him and that would present problems. Trevor wouldn't know where to go. He was certain that he would be arrested for dealing drugs and burglaries he'd committed when he was a teenager. In one of them, he'd gotten violent when the old man whose house he'd broken into attacked him with a baseball bat. Trevor got it away from him, hit the man and knocked him to the ground. He lay motionless. Trevor was petrified that he had killed him. He took off for upstate New York and found the opportunity with the monks.

He'd only taken the job because of the monastery's remoteness. He thought he could hide out here for a year until some of the heat on him cooled down.

That never happened.

Ironically, after twelve years he had a semblance of a life. He'd been a loner since he was a little boy, but over the twelve years he was here, he'd developed a sense of well-being and comfort. If he returned, what would he return to? He would be unskilled, out of touch with what was happening in the world and the only thing he'd face was jail. His mother would be sixty-eight years old, if she were still alive, and they weren't even that close. He might have a brother who was eleven years his senior, but they hadn't been close because of the age difference. He had nothing and no one.

He viewed himself as a prisoner with a life sentence. He found his pleasures and blocked out the misery.

The first few years were hell for him. He was twenty-five years younger than the handful of other normal-sized people there and they were all bitter about their fates.

There was no air conditioning in the summer, no heat in the winter other than from the fireplace. He had to learn outdoor survival skills: how to hunt, how to use a bow and arrow, how to fish, how to start a fire, how to grow food. The monks sent the normal-sized people basic supplies like toiletry articles and clothing. Despite that, they were cut off from the world. It was like living in the nineteenth century.

Trevor and the nine others he lived with also shared a portion of the eastern territory with Damian and Pete. The other half of the eastern section was occupied by six giants and twelve normal-sized people; eight women and four men. They were led by a giant named Martin, who was twenty-four, considered middle-aged for giants. He had been the reason the giants and abnormals split up. Damian's uncle Pete had been the leader, but as he grew older, he was challenged by Martin. It was decided that the two groups would lead separate lives. Just as Trevor became the go-between with the monks, he assumed the same role with Martin and his group.

Like every one who'd come before him, Trevor thought of escaping, but he eventually learned the folly of such a thing happening.

The St. Alban's monks had fortified an area within the nature reserve. Not the current crop, but their brethren from the end of the nineteenth century when it was just a huge forest. Their primary obligation had been to contain the giants. What the monks had constructed was actually quite impressive. They hollowed out the caves to accommodate the giants' size and they did the same when the abnormals, as the

58

giants had always called them, started to trickle in, beginning with Nigel Folquist.

The monks built three stone walls, each forty feet high, adjacent to the eastern face of Hammerhead Mountain. They planted huge evergreen trees to conceal the barriers. There was only one door, which gave the monks entrance on the rare occasion that they had to go inside. It was built only for normal-sized persons. The only way out for a giant would be to climb the wall which was impossible because of the sleekness of the mountain.

As the years passed and people stumbled into the reserve, the monks, being Christian men of faith, gave everyone a choice: stay here, and live out your life, or die.

Every one chose life, and as the giants did, they had all accepted their fate eventually that they would never get out.

With the passage of time, most of the giants mated and had a child or two. The children grew up and mated with another. And on and on it progressed until 1971 when a disease wiped out seventy-five percent of them. Strangely, the abnormal-sized people all survived.

The 1971 scourge also killed off most of the childbearing females. The last giant baby to be born was Damian.

Assuming that Damian lived a normal life, the giants would be officially gone upon his death.

~~~~~~

In the dozen years Trevor had lived with the giants, he had changed. The recklessness that plagued him during his formative years was gone. He had grown up and become a responsible adult. Over the years, the monks left him alone and gave him responsibilities. If a giant died or got sick, he told them. If someone new had the misfortune to find him or herself trapped in the reserve, he was the one who informed them that they could never leave. When a normal-sized person died or took seriously ill and needed hospital care, he knew it would be the end for them. The monks' policy of no one ever leaving resulted in numerous deaths over the last 100-plus years.

He had learned that the hard way when he broke his leg at the age of 21, when he considered himself a runner. He knew he needed medical care, that it needed to be set, but the monks wouldn't let him out or call a doctor. So, the leg had to heal on its own, leaving him with a hideous limp and incredible pain if he walked too fast. For all intent and purpose, he was crippled. He used a cane, which he made for himself. He moved like an old man. Some of the elderly abnormals could walk faster than he.

Trevor was in his garden pruning his tomato plants when he heard the reverberation of footsteps approaching. He looked up and saw Pete coming.

"Hey," he said.

Pete crouched down as he always did when communicating to Trevor.

"There's been a plane crash in the reserve."

"First time in a long time."

"Damian found it," said Pete. "The pilot and two passengers are dead. There's one survivor."

"Where's the wreckage?"

"In Jawbone ravine near Martin's camp in the eastern section. Damian buried it."

Trevor nodded. "Was there smoke?"

"I don't know. I figured you and I could go and check it out. Make sure it's the best place for it to be hidden. You know how he doesn't always complete his jobs."

"He's a kid. Don't be so hard on him. Who's the survivor?"

"A girl."

"How old?"

"My guess is that she's a teenager. She could be about Damian's age."

Trevor perked up. It had been four years since he'd had someone his size to talk to, to find out about what had happened in the world. He wasn't allowed newspapers or magazines. Since the three mountain climbers showed up four years ago, time had stood still for him.

"Her clothes were ripped and dirty. Can you spare some pants and a shirt?"

"Sure." The monks had always been generous with providing clothing for Trevor and the other normal-sized captives.

Trevor smiled. "I can't tell you how much I need to talk to someone who's been out in the world. Can you understand that?"

Pete nodded yes, even though he didn't understand, not really. Living in the reserve was the only world he knew. Ever since Trevor had arrived all he talked about was finding out what was happening in the real world. To Pete, where they were living was the real and only world. He didn't care about anything outside.

Trevor nodded and said, "Let me get some first-aid supplies and we'll go."

He went inside his cave and got two shirts and a pair of jeans. He also grabbed some socks, making a mental note to ask the monks for more, then retrieved the first aid kit. He came back outside.

Pete blurted something that bothered Trevor.

"I think she might be a runner."

"Based on what?" Trevor asked.

"Instinct."

"That's a concern. Did you tell her about the monks and their rules? And the Catholic Church?"

"Not yet."

"What about Damian? You know what a big mouth he has."

Pete nodded in agreement. "I don't think he had time. I was hoping you would be the one to handle that. She's still in shock over seeing giants."

"Alright. I'll do it."

"If she's not injured, you should make room for her with the women."

Trevor nodded in agreement.

He wondered if she was good-looking.

CHAPTER

8

Damian filled the human-sized cup, which Trevor used when he visited, with water he stored in a huge barrel. He had also picked two apples and three pears from the orchard. After nearly two days, Juliet would be ravenous. He finally heard her stir and utter a moan, so he peered into the bedroom. He knocked on the door. She looked up.

"May I come in?"

"Yes."

He says "may," not "can."

How did he learn to speak like an Englishman?

"I brought you a bite to eat."

"Thank you."

She hungrily grabbed the cup of water and downed all of it, then she took all five pieces of fruit and began scarfing an apple.

She wished she had a Starbucks strawberry macchiato.

"You probably want to clean yourself up when you finish," said Damian."

"Yeah. I feel pretty grungy."

"I can bring you water or, if you like, there's a stream nearby if you'd like a proper bath."

"Thank you. Bring me the water for now."

Damian nodded yes. As he watched Juliet start on the second apple, he realized he had neglected asking what her name was.

She glanced up in his direction.

"You're a giant."

"Yes."

"How tall are you?"

"I don't know exactly. About sixteen feet." He crouched down and got closer.

"Thank you for saving me," she said.

"You're welcome."

They stared at each other silently for several seconds, taking each other in.

He's so handsome.

She's so pretty.

His voice is so deep and cool.

Her hair is beautiful and her skin is so soft.

He'd never seen blonde hair before.

"I don't know why, but I'm not afraid of you," she said.

"I could say the same thing," he said.

They both laughed.

Juliet said, "Why would you be afraid of me?"

"I don't know. What's your name?"

"Juliet Pine. I know your name is Damian. I heard that first giant say it. Do you have a last name?"

"Maybe."

She looked at him with a confused expression.

"My official name is number six-forty-seven."

"I don't understand."

"It's how I'm identified as a giant," he said. "Six-forty-seven. My uncle Paul is five-sixty-one."

"Why a number?"

"Every giant whoever was here had a number. Six-forty-seven is the last one. We called ourselves proper names, but we never had surnames."

"Does that mean you're the last giant?"

"Yes."

"Wow. How did you get named Damian?"

He shrugged his shoulders. "Me mum liked it, I guess."

"The other giant you chased away is named Victor."

"Yes. How'd you know?"

"I heard you call him by name."

"He lives in a different territory. Can you lift up your arms?"

"I think so." Juliet lifted both arms. The right side hurt, but she could do it.

"How about your legs?"

Juliet lifted her legs. "I think I rammed into something when we crashed. I'm a little sore. That's all. I can move."

"You're lucky. The people with you weren't. "He stopped himself. "Are you sure they're dead?"

"Yes."

"Trevor will look at you. He's good at these things."

She had to ask him. "Who is Trevor?"

"My friend."

"Is he a giant?"

"No. He's an abnormal."

There's that word again.

"Is he a doctor, Damian?"

"No, but he knows stuff about health. Once you recover, you can live with Trevor and the abnormals he takes care of."

I will not be living with anybody here.

"How many are there?"

"Nine. Well, ten including him."

"Why does he take care of them?"

"They're old, sick."

"Do they live in a cave too?"

"Yes. Caves are the only places we can live.'

"Why don't you all live together?"

Damian smiled. "Because we're too big and they're too small. It's easier if we don't live too near each other. I almost stepped on Trevor a bunch of time. I could've killed him. And then there's the matter of the feud."

"What do you mean?"

"My uncle is kind of a pain, kind of a curmudgeon, but he's a good bloke. He used to be the leader of the giants. then he got, well, overthrown."

"Who by?"

"You mean "by whom?"

He's right. This giant just corrected my grammar.

"Martin. He's younger than Uncle Pete. He banished us from the main group when I was nine because he didn't like my uncle's way of doing things, but we didn't care. We tried to educate them, but Martin didn't want it. It's like, we're educated and they're not. We've lived separately ever since. Sometimes we run into each other when we're hunting for food. Like today."

That's what the bow and arrow is for.

"You hunt?"

"Yes. Every day. For Uncle Pete, myself and for our abnormals, but mainly I farm. I'm harvesting now, preparing for the winter. I also use the bow and arrow for protection."

Protection from what?

"From...?"

"It's dangerous in the reserve, especially at night. You don't want to be outside of your cave at night."

The statement unsettled Juliet.

"If I wouldn't have been with you, would you have talked to the other giant?" she asked.

"No. I can't stand him. He and his brother used to pick on me until I grew up. He's afraid of me now, they all are."

"Why can't you just get along?"

"I don't know. It's stupid. We're all spread out here. If your plane would've gone down in another section, I would never have found you. You were lucky today was a bad hunting day, otherwise I wouldn't have been in the section where you crashed. One of Martin's giants would have found you or maybe nobody would have and you would've died. We rarely see Martin or any of them. It's pretty much my uncle, Trevor's people and me. The giant you saw is harmless. He was probably hunting for his dinner. They always wander off their territory and into ours. I don't care. Live and let live."

"Your uncle didn't seem as nice as you."

"He's sick. He's..." He almost said that his uncle was dying, but decided against it.

"Do you have a mother and father? I mean, I know you have parents, but where are they?"

"My father died when I was six. My mother died four years ago."

"My mom passed away last year," said Juliet. "It's just me, my brother Greg and my dad now. Do you have any other relatives besides your uncle?"

"No."

"You said there were other giants. You're not related to them?"

"No. We all had different families. Some were related, others weren't. I wasn't born when over half of us died. Each year there are fewer of us. I'm the youngest and the last giant."

The remark unsettled Juliet.

"What is this place?" she asked. "I mean, there are giants here. Giants! Why? How can that be? How did you get here? Why haven't you escaped? Why doesn't the world know about you? You can talk. You're intelligent. It's incredible. I thought it was a dream, but now I know it's not. It's like being in another world. A world of giants. What I don't understand is why you're here in this forest. It doesn't make sense."

"The Catholic Church put us here a long time ago. In the nineteenth century. In eighteen seventy-two."

The Catholic Church?

"Why?"

"To hide us from the world. There's no mention of us in the history books. That's because of the Catholic Church."

Juliet stared at Damian, confused.

"I don't understand."

"Wait for Trevor. He can answer better than me."

"If you say so."

"You'll like him. He's very smart."

"If he can answer my questions, I'll like him a lot."

"And once you recover, you can live with Trevor and the other abnormals."

Live with him?

"Why do I have to live with him? Actually, why would I have to live with anybody? I'm obviously going to be rescued. I mean, I was in a plane that crashed. Somebody will be looking for me."

Damian looked at her with sadness in his eyes. Then, softly, he said, "But they won't find you."

"But... "

Not ever."

She stared at Damian. He saw her eyes fill with tears.

"I'm sorry, Juliet."

Juliet felt sick to her stomach. She thought she might throw up.

CHAPTER

9

Greg Pine had been unable to sleep for the last day-and-a-half, ever since Juliet hadn't called him or returned his calls. She was supposed to phone when she landed at Plattsburg International Airport. This wasn't like her. She was more responsible. He was bad with time, constantly missed appointments, always late. His dad liked to say that he was always a day late and a dollar short. And he had a bad temper, which he was always trying to contain. He wondered if he had irritated the police chief he'd spoken to.

When Greg found out that Juliet had never arrived at the airport, he became apoplectic.

Greg decided not to call his father until he'd found out some facts. He was dealing with a flooded house back in Denver. That Juliet was missing would only add to his misery. Instead, he called Habitat America. He learned that they had been in contact with people at LaGuardia and Plattsburg Airports, but had heard only that Juliet's plane had stopped all communication while flying near the Cassoulet Nature Reserve in upstate New York.

"Be patient," someone told him. "We'll get to the bottom of what happened."

Greg had been on the phone for close to two hours looking for the right people to talk to and ask questions. David Parterro, the Chief of Police of Keene, New York had put him off, pleading he hadn't even heard of a plane going down.

He was getting nowhere.

While at the front desk of the hotel where he was staying, a clerk overheard him and offered assistance.

"Excuse me, Mister Pine?"

That someone called him "Mister Pine" unsettled Greg because he was wearing jeans, sandals and a Denver Bronco's hoodie.

"Uh, yes?" he said.

"I couldn't help but hear you mention the Cassoulet Reserve. The hotel uses a tour guide up there who might be able to help you. I can't promise anything, though."

He reached for a brochure among several on a stand by the front desk and handed it to Greg.

"There's a phone number at the bottom, Mister Pine."

PURDELL TOURS

ED PURDELL

KING OF THE ADIRONDACKS

OVER LAND IN A VAN

AND BY AIR, ANYWHERE

"How would this person get news?" Greg asked.

"He's always looking for business. He knows all the local busybodies and stays in touch with shops and tourist attractions up there. He might have heard something. Maybe not, but it's worth a try."

Greg was skimming the brochure as he listened.

"And he's gotten lots of positive reviews from our customers, but I should warn you. He can come off as, well, colorful."

"How do you know?"

"He's driven down to New York a few times to drop off new brochures. He's one of those bigger-than-life types."

"If he can help me find my sister, I don't care how colorful he is."

He looked at the phone number and dialed.

CHAPTER

10

"**W**hat do you mean they won't ever find me?" Juliet crunched into the second pear.

"Trevor will explain."

Anxious and with a full mouth, Juliet said, "I don't want to wait for Trevor. Why can't *you* explain?"

"Because there's a lot to tell," said Damian. "He'll do it better. You asked me why you can't stay with me. You're a young girl. You shouldn't be alone. You need to be with other people, but mainly for safety."

"Safety from what?"

"You're livin' in a forest filled with animals. Some are dangerous. They prowl at night."

Oh my God!

"And the other giants may be a danger to you."

Oh my God!

"They're rough around the edges."

"But you said they all sound British!"

"They do, but that's all: they *sound* British. They don't use their heads. Most are twits. They might kidnap you."

Would they turn me into a sex slave?

"You're scaring me."

"There's safety in numbers," he said.

"But you were by yourself when you rescued me?"

"I can take care of myself. I don't think you can."

He's right about that.

"If they kidnapped me what would they do with me?" she asked.

"Make you work for them."

"Doing what?"

"Cooking. They need a cook."

"Why would they assume I know how to cook?"

"You're a female. Females cook."

"I don't cook. If it can't be microwaved or toasted, I'm helpless in the kitchen."

"One of the abnormals will teach you."

"I don't think so." She changed the subject. "You said you and your parents were educated. How did that happen? I mean, you talk so well and you're intelligent. I thought giants just grunted. That Victor giant could talk too, I mean, not as well as you, but he could communicate. And..." She hesitated for a few seconds. "And why do you sound like you come from England?"

He smiled again. "The first abnormal person was a British mountain climber who was also a school teacher. He got stuck here because of an earthquake. A small one that opened up the rocks he was climbing. He taught English to a bunch of the early giants when they were kids. Then the people he taught, taught others and so on. Some wanted to learn, some didn't. My mother taught me, her mother taught her, her mother taught her and it was like that for most families."

"It's so strange. When I think of giants, I never think of them being in families. I never thought of them as real, either, but in stories, they're always sort of... loners. And monsters."

"The second teacher was a mail delivery pilot whose plane went down in 1923. Dickie Aimler. He was Australian, which is basically the same as being British. Nigel taught the nineteenth century giants to speak the Kings English and Dickie taught his giants Australian slang and how to tell stories. He told my ancestors every detail of his life and the lives of his friends and pretty much everyone he knew. He had his giants tell the stories of their lives. When Trevor got stuck here he really helped me learn. He read to me from books he got from the monks, all kinds of books. Do you know what oral histories are?"

"Slaves used them to pass on family histories," said Juliet. "That's pretty much all I know. Do you know what slaves are? Were?"

"Yes. It was the same with the giants. We were like slaves."

Oh my God!

"How many giants live here?"

"Eleven. There used to be hundreds."

"What happened to the others?"

"They died."

The remark hung in the air.

"At one time there were giants livin' throughout the world. In private enclaves. They didn't bother anyone. Then in the fifteenth century something happened, an outbreak that wiped out two thirds of them. In the nineteen century there was another plague that killed only the adult giants. For some reason the child giants were spared."

Child giants?

"The Vatican knew about the giants, but let them live as long as they stayed contained. The Pope at the time could not see killing children, even though they were giants who would grow up. So, they shipped them here to America in the late nineteenth century. This area was remote and unapproachable. Child giants were manageable, but fifteen, eighteen-foot adults? My father was nineteen-feet tall. How could they round them up and get them here safely?"

"I was wondering about that," said Juliet.

"Children could be controlled better because of their

size. They all were brought here when they were children, five or six feet tall. When they grew up, they mated. And here we are, what's left of us. By the time I was born there were about forty-five left. One by one they all died. There were none left for me to find a mate or to have children with."

"Sorry."

"You're the first girl I ever met."

He's blushing. That's so cute.

She smiled at him and extended her hand. "Nice to meet you, Damian."

He touched her hand with his right index finger.

"Nice to meet you, Juliet."

Now he's really blushing.

"If you want, you can ask me more questions," he said.

"Okay." She hesitated for several seconds. "Where is this Cassoulet Reserve located?"

"On the fringe of the Adirondack Mountain range right next to St. Alban's Monastery. It's run by the Catholic Order of Cistercians of the Strict Observance. You might know them as Trappists."

"I've heard of Trappist monks, but I don't know anything about them."

"This group is known for its production and marketing of Smiling Monk Preserves, which partially supports the abbey. Ever heard of them?"

"No. I don't eat sugar. How did the abnormal people get here?"

"They had the bad luck to get imprisoned in this place," said Damian.

"You mean like me? Having the pilot lose control of the plane?"

"Different ways. Accidents. Natural disturbances. Hikers. Yours is the sixteenth plane to crash over the years. It's always the small ones. The first pilot to crash was Dickie. May sixth."

"How do you know the exact date?" Juliet asked.

"I remember the dates of things that rarely happen. The first five crashes were either daredevils or mail carriers. They died. Dickie stayed here for forty-two years. Some crashes had survivors who were rescued."

Juliet perked up. "Then why can't I be rescued?"

"When these planes crashed everybody on them was alive," said Damian. "They were in good condition and the pilot could radio for help. And they landed in a different section from where the giants lived. In your case, everyone was dead except you and the plane was going to blow up."

Juliet considered what Damian said. "How did Trevor wind up here?"

"He witnessed a small earthquake and was kept here."

"That makes no sense."

"There's an old cemetery on the northern side, where the entrance is. The ground was ripped up and he saw the remains of two giants. They don't bury the giants anymore."

"What do they do with them?"

"They burn the bodies in a pit. It's much simpler."

"What about the abnormals?"

"The last people to get stuck here was four years ago," said Damian. "Three mountain climbers were on the other side of the ridge when there was a tremor. Trevor called it a fissure. For the mountain climbers it opened up a fissure and plunked them inside with us with no way to escape."

"So, they're here now too."

"Only one is. The other two are dead. They were runners, which means they tried to escape. They tried to run. They failed. They were eliminated."

"You mean they died."

"I mean they were caught and *killed*."

"By who?"

"One man. Over the years, he was replaced by a different man, but it was always one man. He works for The Vatican."

The Vatican?

"He's a Knight Templar."

"I thought Knight Templars were good men who protected the Church like five hundred years ago." She remembered that from a religion course she took.

"That's what they are," said Damian. "It's what they do. They protect this place from the world."

"You mean the Pope knows about this place?"

"Yes. Trevor told me the current Templar uses helicopters."

"How would Trevor know?"

"He made friends with a monk," said Damian. "His name is Brother Samuel. They talk sometimes. He's the one Trevor deals with when he needs supplies or one of the giants dies."

"Why when a giant dies?"

"They keep records."

"For what?"

"They're counting down until the last giant, me, dies and it will all be over."

"I don't understand," said Juliet

"To the monks we don't have names."

"You have numbers?"

Damian nodded his head yes.

"Do you mean that there were six hundred-forty-seven giants that have lived here?

"Yes."

Damian wanted to tell her about the giants of Mont Blanc in France who he believed still existed, but decided not to. He would wait for a better time, after she settled in.

"Anyway, in one of their gossip sessions, Brother Samuel said that the Knight Templar uses things called Black Ops when they need something taken care of," said Damian. "They saw the mountain climbers trying to escape up Hammerhead Mountain. They called him. He arrived with Black Op helicopters and shot them."

What's with these monks?

"I can't believe the monks are the bad guys," she said. "What the hell?"

"Abbot Gassner is the one who calls the Templar when he's needed. You have to see it from their point of view. They were given a job by the Catholic Church. They were told to contain the giants no matter what and that's what they've been doing."

"Wouldn't you rather be free?"

Damian hesitated. "I don't know what that means, luv. All I know about freedom is what Trevor told me. He told me about the freedom *he* had before he got here. He described it by saying it was like being a bird who could fly wherever he wanted. He said there were rules that people had to follow, but that if you were a good person you could find peace. I couldn't have it because I'm so big. I could never be free like Trevor was or like you were. I'm tall, but I wish I were an abnormal. Abnormals can lead normal lives. They all adapted and stopped trying to run."

"And there's no way out?"

Damian shook his head no.

"And if I understand you correctly, you're telling me that I will have to live here for the rest of my life. Is that right, Damian?"

He hesitated. "Yes."

Oh my God! I can't do this! There's got to be a way out of here!

Juliet remembered what she'd overheard Damian say to his uncle about death being better than the life she would have here. And now, hearing him tell her that this place would be her new home was just too bizarre and terrifying.

She closed her eyes. She knew one thing for sure. She was going to get out of this place or die trying.

But how?

She bent over with the dry heaves and started to cry.

Damian watched her helplessly. He wished that he were her size or that she were his size so he could comfort her.

She's so sweet

CHAPTER

11

Pete picked Trevor up, flipped him over onto his right shoulder and headed to the Cessna's burial site in the ravine. Despite his age and health, carrying Trevor was a snap and Pete still moved considerably fast.

They walked in silence. Pete wasn't much of a talker and Trevor loved to shoot the breeze, but in the twelve years they'd known each other, Trevor came to respect Pete's space. He learned a long time ago that if Pete had something to say, he would say it; otherwise, he kept his thoughts to himself.

When they got to where Damian had buried the plane, they were satisfied that he'd done a decent job.

"Looks good," said Trevor as he walked around the covered hole. "But it needs some touching up."

Damian had put enough branches, shrubs and rocks over the spot where the plane was, but up close, Pete could tell that something was hidden there.

"Spread out some of the shrubbery on it," said Pete. "And maybe place a few more rocks around it and some more dirt."

Trevor nodded and did as he was instructed. Within five minutes he was done.

"No one could ever find it now," said Pete. "Let's go." He lowered his right arm. "Get on." Trevor climbed onto Pete's hand and he put him back on his shoulder.

They moved on, back to the cave and Juliet. To Trevor's surprise, Pete started a conversation.

"I worry about what will happen to Damian when I'm gone. He'll be alone."

"He'll have me," said Trevor. "We'll have each other. And you'll be around for years."

"I don't think so," Pete said soberly. "He won't have me to keep him on a leash. I'm afraid he's going to do something stupid."

"Run?"

"Yes."

"Don't worry, Pete. I've had lots of conversations about running with him. I've talked him out of it."

"Sometimes he asks me to go over the oral history."

Trevor sighed. "He believes that it's true. He needs to believe it."

"We all needed to believe it when we're young," said Pete. "If only his mother hadn't given him that ring. I think Damian believes in that damn thing more than that there are giants in France. She said his destiny is..."

"To be a leader," Trevor interrupted. "He brings that up with me too. I talk him out of believing. I can understand how when he first heard it, he might believe it, but not anymore. Progress and inventiveness have changed the world. I can't imagine what the world is like out there now, after twelve years. I'm afraid that if Damian tried to escape and actually attempted to make his way to France, he wouldn't get more than a mile away before they got him."

"I have the same fear," said Pete.

"We won't have to worry. This place has no way out. Every time I look at my foot and my leg, I know that to be true."

CHAPTER

12

Edward Purdell had been obsessed with giants since he was eight years old when he'd seen the remains of one. That was fifty-six years ago. He had to constantly remind himself that not everyone believed in giants at the same level that he did.

He was the organizer of a small, worldwide network of giant hunters who believed as strongly as he did in the existence of them. Most of its members were up in years and lived primarily in France and Germany where there'd been sightings of giants. The Frenchmen believed Mont Blanc held giants, the group's African member believed they were near Mount Kilimanjaro and a handful of northern Europeans swore they were in The Black Forest.

"Young kids just aren't interested in giants," Edward would say. "They don't believe. I don't get it."

There was only one local person in the group, Teddy Germaine, Edward's business partner. He was a pilot who handled all the air excursions for Edward's touring company. They went in together after first connecting as giant hunters.

Teddy was sixty-five years old. He'd gotten a twenty-eight-second glimpse of a giant's face in Cassoulet Reserve looking up at him when he was thirty-seven. He was a freelance flight instructor at Plattsburg Airport. On occasion, a student would lose control of the aircraft and drift the plane over the reserve. Teddy would have to take the yoke and veer it back on course. One sunny morning, a sixteen-year-old boy panicked and the plane went careening over the reserve. Teddy saw the giant's face while he was guiding the plane back to safety.

For years, he'd heard the occasional tale from other pilots of planes that flew too low over the reserve. A minor glance into the trees would occasionally lead to a sighting, however minimal, of movement.

Large movement.

A face or a hand or two hands reaching out above the treetops. He had even talked to a few pilots who had sightings, but nothing came of it.

Teddy became an instant believer and sought out Edward who had regaled him with his giant stories for years.

Teddy and Edward would get together every few months to talk about the latest findings on giants on the Internet, but there weren't many sightings. Their get-togethers were more of an excuse to have a few drinks and carry on about what they would do if they found access to Cassoulet Reserve, than accomplishing anything.

As Teddy liked to say, "People don't give a damn. It's all Hollywood's fault with their shitty movies and special effects."

But he still believed and so did Edward because they had no choice—-they had seen proof of giants.

Edward's father was an amateur dinosaur hunter, looking for dinosaur bones in Northern Canada. He always brought Edward with him. One day they stumbled upon a find at a newly discovered mound: a human giant remains! It measured thirteen feet and seven inches. It was just he and his father digging. Mister Purdell had neglected to bring a camera, so he left Edward with the remains as he made the two-hour drive to their home to get a camera.

As an eight-year-old, his curiosity got the best of him, so Edward touched the head of the giant and to his horror, the entire thing disintegrated. When his father returned there was nothing. But the experience set in motion a career choice. "I know there are giants," he said. "And I will find one and show the world."

He kept what he saw to himself at first, but over the last thirty years, especially since the Internet was invented, he found others like himself throughout the world.

But no one took the sightings seriously. It was like people who claimed to have seen UFOs. The general public needed proof. Since Edward had nothing concrete, he knew that the best evidence would be a giant, in the flesh.

Edward had always thought that if he could find a way to gain access to the reserve, he would be able to spot a giant. When he was a younger man, he managed to get inside on three occasions at the southern, northern and western perimeters of Cassoulet Reserve, but getting in was too easy. Once inside, Hammerhead Mountain was too jagged and steep to climb down. He had no choice but to return. He began to suspect that the eastern perimeter was the place to enter, but it was impossible to gain access there.

He suspected that the monks knew something or were protecting something because getting anywhere near the eastern section was undoable. A mountain range prevented anything from getting near the area making the only entrance to the region from the grounds of the abbey. The presence of the monks made it impenetrable. They had vineyards against the fenced-in nature preserve.

He supposed that the monks were hiding giants because of an incident in the local newspaper more than thirty-five years ago. A monk had, for lack of a better explanation, lost his mind, wandered off the monastery grounds, made his way to a reporter in the town and proceeded to talk about the giant buried in the cemetery at St. Albans. He also mentioned the living giants who had been kept prisoner since the monastery was founded.

As fate would have it, the reporter he had spoken to was a devout Catholic who thought he was crazy, so instead of reporting what the monk had told her, she called the Monsignor who ran St. Albans back then. He thanked her and quickly came into town and took him back. In the article that appeared in the paper, there was no mention of the buried or living giants.

Ironically, the reporter was found dead one week later. Her death was identified as an accident, but Edward always suspected that she had been silenced.

By whom, he wasn't sure, but he had an idea. He didn't know the person's name, but he was aware of the organization he belonged to.

The Knights Templar.

The organization supposedly didn't exist anymore, but Edward suspected it did and knew that the monk was right.

At sixty-four he was still that eight-year-old child who accidentally destroyed the giant he and his father had found.

And he was still looking.

~~~~~~

Edward's phone rang. He picked it up.

"Purdell Tours," he said. "Over land in a van and by air anywhere. This is Edward Purdell, the proprietor. How may I help you?

Greg cleared his throat. "My name is Greg Pine. I need to get into, or I need someone to get into, Cassoulet Reserve. My sister is missing. She went down in a plane crash two days ago. Can you help me?"

Edward crinkled his nose. "I haven't heard of any plane crashes in the area for the last two days or even the last four months or even the last four years."

"Maybe the authorities don't know it's there yet, but I know her plane went down either in the reserve or near it."

"How do you know, Mister Pine."

"I don't really. I just think so. I hope so."

"So then this isn't a rescue mission. This is a recovery operation."

The remark unsettled Greg. "No. It's a rescue."

"Do you know for a fact that your sister's plane crashed?"

"It's the only explanation. The Chief of Police of Keene assured me that if the plane went down, they would know about it, but it's a small plane. I feel it in my bones that it crashed."

Edward knew he had the chance to make some fast money and money was always something he needed, so upon hearing Greg Pine's statement, he shifted into high gear. He also smelled an opportunity to gain access to the reserve.

"All right. Very well. Understand that the reserve covers a lot of land. Do you have any idea which section she would've flown over?"

"I didn't know there were any sections," said Greg.

"North, South, East and West. Have you tried talking to the monks?"

"What monks?"

"The monks who own the land surrounding the reserve. Let me tell you about the monks. They come across as very friendly and kind, and frankly, they are. But when it comes to gaining entrance to the reserve, they get strange."

"Strange how?" Greg asked.

"Secretive. They've controlled the reserve for over a hundred-and-fifty years. They act like they're hiding something?"

Greg was suspicious. "What would they be hiding?"

Edward was tempted to bring up the giants, but decided it was too soon. This guy was worried about finding his sister. Now wasn't the time to broach the subject of giants. He had to be careful before introducing the topic wherever he went. He knew that it was easy to turn off people with his exuberance.

"Why would the monks control part of the reserve?" Greg asked.

"It hasn't always been a reserve. They were here first, when it was just a forest. When the country became environmentally aware and started setting aside forest areas for preservation, they worked something out with the government. If you needed to get into the western, northern and southern sectors it wouldn't be a problem; but whenever there's a need to get into the eastern section, the monks object."

"Are you telling me that if they know a plane has crashed in that part of the reserve, they would do nothing about it?"

"Let's just say that investigation wouldn't be encouraged."

"That makes no sense."

Greg sat back in his chair, uncomfortable. He felt that he'd been given the runaround by Captain Parterro. Maybe this guy was right. "Can I contact the monks directly?"

"You can, but don't expect much cooperation."

What Edward wanted to say was *"Because their job is to protect the giants."*

Edward's mind was racing. If he could get into the reserve under the pretense of looking for this guy's sister, he might have an opportunity to find a giant. First, he would need to find out if a plane had been reported as crashed or missing and then if the Federal Safety Review Board was investigating. That would be easy because he had enough connections at the local airport to get this information with a phone call.

"Here's what I can do for you," said Edward. "Let me make a couple of calls. If there's a report of a crashed or missing plane we might have a way to get inside. If not, the best I can do for you is provide you with a flight tour."

"What's that?"

"My partner Teddy will fly you around Cassoulet Reserve, but I'll tell him to take a little detour."

"I googled the reserve," said Greg. "It's supposed to be a no-flyover zone."

"Do you want to find a crashed plane or not?" said Edward curtly.

"Oh. Yes. Yes, I do."

"Then I have to break some rules. Understand what I'm saying?"

"Yes. Break as many as you need to."

"I'll make my calls now. You should get a flight up here to Plattsburg Airport. Try to get here first thing tomorrow. I'll pick you up."

"Alright."

"But first, we need to discuss my fee."

CHAPTER

13

When they got back to the cave, Pete put Trevor down and they walked into the room where Juliet was. She had fallen asleep again. Damian was watching her, listening to her breath, fascinated by her beauty.

Trevor acknowledged Damian with a nod, then approached Juliet. Like Damian, he too couldn't take his eyes off of her.

She's beautiful!

She was the first young girl he'd seen since he got here twelve years ago.

He wished that he had freshened up and at least shaved, not that it would have helped. He knew that the time he'd spent in the reserve had aged him. He was only thirty-one, but he looked ten years older. He had requested moisturizer from the monks, but had been denied. On the other hand, he was in excellent shape because of the vegetarian diet he'd been living on. He was all muscle.

Pete spoke up. "Wake her, Trevor."

"I can't take my eyes off her," Trevor said as he set down the clothes he'd brought for her. "She's incredible. Damian, this is the kind of girl I told you about."

Trevor approached Juliet slowly, almost reverentially, and gently nudged her right shoulder. Once, twice, three times. She stirred momentarily, then woke up, startled and sleepy-eyed.

Upon seeing a normal-sized adult, she relaxed. She smiled.

I was dreaming after all. I knew this couldn't be true.

He looked to be not much taller than she and was extremely thin, but was in excellent shape.

"Thank God," Juliet said. "I dreamt that I was in a place populated by giants and that one of them saved me. I mean, I was actually talking to a giant."

"You *were*," said Trevor.

"What?"

"Get used to it," Trevor said firmly. "They'll be your friends from now on. So, will I. There are others here who are your size. We all stick together. We all pitch in and do what we can to survive."

She noticed the odd way he was looking at her. He was half-grinning and had a crazy glint in his eyes. It made her uncomfortable.

"I need to ask you about that," she said. "Damien said that I'll never be able to leave this place."

"That's correct."

Juliet was suddenly frightened again. She adjusted herself and sat up. "Why is that? It strikes me as being very unfair."

"Because you know that there are giants here. No one is supposed to know that."

"Damian said the same thing. I don't understand."

"Why do you think I'm here? I found out about them when I was nineteen."

"How old are you now?"

"How old do I look?"

She looked closely at his face. "I don't know, about forty-five, forty-six."

The comment bothered him. "I'll be thirty-two years old in two months."

Juliet was taken aback and embarrassed. He looked so much older.

"Twelve years you've been here?" she said, totally shocked. "Why didn't you try to escape?"

Trevor smiled ruefully. "I did. Everybody tries, but succeeding is another story. We can get into that later. We'll have plenty of time to talk and get to know each other better."

Get to know each other better?

Is this guy hitting on me?

"First, it's a pleasure to meet you. My name is Trevor. Trevor Bruckner"

100

A pleasure to meet me? Is he nuts?

She decided it would be smart to follow his lead.

"Juliet Pine."

Trevor extended his right hand. Awkwardly, she shook it. It was moist, clammy.

She could smell him too, like she smelled Damian. But unlike Damian who smelled nice, Trevor smelled like someone who needed a spray of deodorant.

She felt sick to her stomach.

"I need to know how you're feeling, Juliet," Trevor asked.

"My body is just sore from being tossed around in the plane. And my head was killing me, but not anymore. I pretty much missed the crash because I was on medication and out of it. From the way my side feels I think I landed hard on it. My head has a big bump, but it's smaller now. I think I'll be okay. And as far as me never getting out of this place, that's ridiculous. There has to be someone I can talk to. I shouldn't have to stay anywhere I don't want to."

Trevor sighed.

Pete is right. She's a runner.

And she's trouble.

Trevor had dated girls that were trouble. He had difficult time getting along with them. But that was when he was a teenager. He was different now, more patient, understanding and mature. He was convinced that his interminable loneliness would also play a factor in a relationship. He would be unselfish and giving. He had learned how to treat a woman by living without one for a dozen years.

He looked at Juliet with frustration. "We'll see. Let me have a look at your head."

"What do you mean 'we'll see'?"

"We'll talk about that tomorrow or the day after, I promise. Lean forward, please."

She did so. She felt Trevor's boney fingers probing the wound. It made her feel even more awkward.

"Damian said you weren't a doctor."

"I'm not."

"How do you know what to do?"

"Let's just say I picked things up along the way. Your head wound is just a big bump with a tiny cut. You'll be fine. I have something that'll take care of it. Damian, would you get me some water and a towel?"

Damian nodded, glanced at his uncle and left the room.

As Trevor gently squeezed her right arm and leg, Juliet found herself wondering what Damian and Trevor did all day long. How did they spend their time? What did they do for entertainment? Was there anything to do? Where did they get food? What was it like here at night? Damian had told her that nighttime was dangerous. Didn't they ever think about escaping?

Trevor pressed his right-hand fingers into Juliet's side. "That hurt?"

"A little," she said. "Manageable."

He pressed another place. "That?"

"No."

He pressed a third spot. "How about that?"

She jumped! "Ow!" He kept pressing. "That hurts!"

"You're good. Fortunately, you won't need medical attention?"

"Why do you say 'fortunately'?"

"You won't have to go to a hospital."

"I don't understand."

Damian returned with a large bowl of water and a piece of cloth that reminded Juliet of a gigantic beach towel. He set it on the floor between Trevor and Juliet.

As Trevor cleaned Juliet's head wound, he spoke. "Let's say you had a broken leg. You wouldn't be taken to a hospital. You would have to live with it. The pain, the crippled, gimp aspect. You would limp for the rest of your life, assuming gangrene didn't set in, in which case your leg would rot and fall off -- because there's no one here qualified to amputate it – or worse. Understand that you're very lucky not to have any major injuries?"

"That doesn't make any sense, but I think I understand."

Trevor looked at her curiously.

"It's because of the monks, right?" said Juliet.

"You know about them?"

"Damian told me."

Trevor glanced at Damian who looked away.

"I'm, what you could say, is the go-between for the monks and everyone here. I've made friends with one of them. He gives me supplies and books. They aren't all bad."

"Why can't he help you escape?"

"He would be punished. You're not understanding the seriousness of this place."

"What do monks have to do with me? I'm not even Catholic. I survived a plane crash. If they're monks, I would think they would want to help me."

"They've handled collateral damage like you and me before."

"Collateral damage? Can't I talk to someone? Please! Your friend? A monk should be reasonable."

"Get that thought out of your head," Trevor said. "You will not see a monk. Not ever. You will not be talking to a monk."

"But... "

"When it's necessary, I'm the one who talks to them. More often than not, they talk to me. I wait for contact from them. They ring a horn three times when they need to see me. Sometimes I don't hear from them for months. You may not like it, but that's how it is."

"You seem like an okay guy, but you're in here," said Juliet, feeling more and more on edge. "I want to talk to someone out *there*. Wherever *there* is. I have to get out of here. I'm starting college in six weeks. I have plans. My brother is in New York City. He'll be going crazy."

Trevor sighed. He hoped he wasn't being too firm with her because he wanted her to like him.

He decided to take a gentler tone. "I'll tell you where you are. We're in a nature reserve regulated by the government."

"I know that already. Damian told me."

He ignored her. "On three sides is private farmland protected by three walls where the monks raise their crops. The fourth side is a mountain. That's where the caves we live in are. Straight up, it's five hundred feet. Know what that means?"

"No."

"It's impenetrable. It means no one gets out and no one gets in unless it's by accident. Not a soul. Not even a giant can climb it."

"But you got in. And Damian said other people got in too."

"All exceptions. All dumb luck. All *bad* luck! We're prisoners in here until we die. When I got here, I was like you. You want to escape. I *know* you want to escape. I wanted to escape and I tried." He gestured toward his crippled, mangled foot. "This is all I have to show for it. It took me three years before I realized that escaping would never happen."

"So, you *did* become a runner?"

"How do you know about runners?" He glanced at Damian. "What did you tell her?"

"Nothing!" Damian snapped.

"I overheard Damian and his uncle talking about them," she said. "They think I'll be one."

Trevor got a noticeably serious tone. "I hope you won't. You'll die. Four years ago... "

"The mountain climbers who fell into the mountain," she interrupted. "Damian told me. They were killed by a guy who was a Knights Templar."

Trevor glared at Damian angrily. "Did you tell her *everything*?"

"She asked," said Damian.

Trevor rolled his eyes.

"What about the third one?" asked Juliet.

"He's still here, but he's bedridden. He can barely walk. Did something to his back and one of his legs. No hospitals. He might as well be dead."

Juliet was starting to feel nauseous again.

"In the past, the only runners were the giants. On three separate occasions, one would make an escape and manage to get out. Lucky for them, right?"

"I guess."

"No. The problem was each of them had nowhere to go. There were no cars, not that they could fit into a car. There were trains in the vicinity, not that he could get on or fit inside a train car. Their only choice was to walk. Where do they walk to? And they all probably left in broad daylight. Which way do they go? They have no idea. What's north, south, east or west?"

Juliet got caught up in the story. "What would they do?"

"Walk until they were caught. It rarely took them long to find them. Giants, as you've noticed, are huge creatures. They need a lot of food and a lot of room. Where do they find food? Or water. One tried to make his way through splotches of forest along the way, but what would he do when the forest ended? He'd be right back in the open again. When he left, he didn't consider that. In those days this area was all rural. Wide open spaces. A random farmhouse. The person the monks used would hunt them down and bring them back here."

"The Knight Templar." She glanced at Damian. "He told me."

Trevor glared at Damian and shook his head.

"That's so sad that they had nowhere to go," said Juliet.

"It's tragic. But when you put yourself in the monk's place, can't say that I blame them."

"How can you say that?"

"The secret would be out."

"That there were giants in the world? What's wrong with that?"

"It would destroy religion as we know it."

"Why? I think it would be incredible to know that giants exist. What an archeological find! Real, living giants!"

"Not to the Catholic Church. Giants are a big no-no."

"It's the twenty-first century. People wouldn't care. They would want to know."

"We'll have plenty of time to discuss this. You have to rest. Take these pills. One every six hours."

He handed her a vial of white pills.

"I don't want to rest. I want to know what I'm up against."

"The Catholic Church has kept the giants secret for a thousand years plus. They were everywhere, but now they're here. These are the last giants alive in the world today."

The remark stung Juliet. "So, because I know there are giants, I'm not allowed to leave?"

"Yes."

"That's wrong."

"Wrong?" Trevor smirked. "I've been telling myself that for the last twelve years. I lost everything. My family. My dog. My life. I haven't listened to or watched television, seen a movie, heard music or a podcast or an iPod or iPad or played a sport. The only pleasure I get is from reading books. I have to hunt what I eat or grow it or catch it. I'm living like an eighteenth-century farmer. I have to look after the other normal-sized people. I live one day at a time. In the winter, I keep a fire going all the time because it gets so cold. The monks let me read from their library, by candlelight. No electricity."

"Are you kidding me, candlelight?"

"For twelve years. But I've learned to live with it. I've made a life for myself. A very small life, but that's okay because it's better than the alternative."

"How do you go on?"

"One reason. Damien." He turned to his young friend.

"Without him I would be so lonely that I'd throw myself off a mountain. Damian makes being here worthwhile. He's my best friend and I'm his best friend. Weird isn't it? A giant and a normal-sized guy being best friends."

"It is, I guess. I mean, he's just a big person."

"That's right. Lately we haven't been getting along." He turned to Damian again. "Have we?"

"No," Damian grunted.

"Teenage stuff. I'm an adult. He takes his frustrations out on me. I give him room. I remember how it was when I was his age. By the time he's in his twenties he'll be fine. We'll be fine. Won't we, Damian?"

"I guess," Damian said sheepishly.

"I have to ask you something," said Trevor. "It could wait, but since you're basically all right, I see no reason to. Will anyone be looking for you?"

"My brother. We came to New York City together. He'll be trying to find out where I am and he'll call our dad. I'm supposed to be interning with The Habitat Project. They'll probably be looking for me too. And the families of the two other interns who died and the pilot's family. When they realize we're not there, someone will notice and I'm sure they'll want to put out a search party or something."

"They won't find you. Even if the monks let them inside to look, they will never find a trace of the plane or you. You will never be found."

She shuddered and broke into a cold sweat.

Trevor let the remark sink into Juliet's head.

D. B Gilles

"I'll repeat this one more time," he said. "Do not think about *ever* getting out. It'll save you lots of frustration. This place is escape proof. Are we clear?"

"Wouldn't it have been worth it to die trying than to live like you're living here?"

Trevor had never been asked that question. Despite the fact that he had changed from the reprehensible teen he was, he still was fearful of returning. He considered the question for a few seconds then decided to lie. "Maybe, but I never had the opportunity to try. And besides, once you get used to it, being here isn't so bad."

There was something unsettling about the determined way Trevor spoke that concerned Juliet.

She rolled her eyes.

We'll see about that.

Damian observed the look on Juliet's face.

He knew for sure that she was going to run and it scared him because he didn't want to lose her.

"Are we clear, Juliet?" said Trevor. He knew that he would have to talk her out of it at some point, but not now. She would need time. Everything was still raw to her.

Juliet nodded yes, but only to appease him. She'd only just met Trevor, but already knew she hated him.

"The sooner you accept what I'm saying, the easier it will be for you," he said.

"Okay," she lied.

"I'm sorry to be the messenger of this news so soon after you got here, but there is no point in waiting to

110

soften the blow. Get some rest. I'll be back tomorrow to tell you the rules."

"What rules?"

"Tomorrow. Damian? Pete? Let's go."

Juliet noticed that despite his size, Damian and Pete seemed to listen to Trevor as if he were some kind of leader.

Pete stood and walked out of the room. Damian gave Juliet a quick glance and a smile, then followed Trevor out.

"Do you think I was too tough on her?" asked Trevor.

"No," said Pete. "She needed to hear it."

"I hope she won't hate me now or that she won't think of me as the enemy. She has to know I told her everything to make things easier on her."

"Maybe you told her a little too soon," said Damian, barely concealing his frustration. "Did you have to make it seem so bloody hopeless?"

"There was no point in sugarcoating the news."

"I'll talk to her," said Damian. "I'll let her know you have her best interests at heart."

"Would you do that? Really, Damian?"

"I know you like her. I know what you're thinking about her. She would be your companion. That's what you want, isn't it?"

"I want more than that. I want a wife. I want someone to be with and talk to and love. I want someone to have kids with."

The remark shocked Pete. "You would raise children in this world?"

"I want kids." He turned to Damian. "Do you think she'll have me?"

"How would I know?" said Damian. He found himself feeling jealous. Even though he knew he could never have Juliet because of his size, he wanted her in his life.

"I'd appreciate anything you can say to her. Anything."

Damian just stared at Trevor expressionless. Trevor knew that look. It meant that Damian was brewing inside, which meant he would give Trevor the cold shoulder. He needed to stifle the mood.

"Let's not be mad at each other," said Trevor. "Can't we put our rift aside and try to welcome this girl into our world. Okay?"

Damian hesitated for several seconds, then halfheartedly said, "Okay."

"The pills I gave her will make her sleep for several hours. When she's healed, I'll bring her over to my compound. I'll tell the women to start making a space."

Damian nodded.

"Do you want me to carry you home?" said Damian.

"No. I'll walk. See you tomorrow."

He walked out of the cave, hoping for a fresh start with Juliet.

CHAPTER

14

As he limped along the trail that led to his cave, Trevor felt happy. And hopeful. He had never thought that a girl or woman would be in the cards for him. He hadn't thought of escaping his fate for eight years. He had shut it out.

Trevor recalled the day that he had been sentenced to live his life in the reserve.

He had only started working as a groundskeeper at St. Alban's Monastery and Retreat House out of desperation. He had needed a temporary place to hide.

"Your primary duties are to tend to the grass, trees and shrubbery," said Brother David. "There is an old cemetery that also needs looking after. Go in there once every couple of weeks. Many of the graves are from the nineteenth or early twentieth century, and they're primarily of our brethren, so rarely will anyone be coming to pay their respects. But on the occasion that someone does, remove the random flowers or wreath that a mourner left."

Trevor had done some research on the profession and learned that a more dignified word for the same responsibilities was *sexton.* He looked up the word in the dictionary and memorized the definition: a church officer or employee who takes care of the church property and at some churches rings the bell for services and digs graves.

He doubted he would be digging any graves. From the looks of the old cemetery no one had been laid to rest in years, in decades it seemed. His supervisor had taken him through a locked wooden door twelve feet high and a foot thick to have access to the old cemetery.

"Trim the weeds and the grass. We're having visitors tomorrow. An elderly cardinal from Spain will be paying respects to his third cousin or something so we want the area to look presentable."

This area where the old cemetery was located was rather imposing. The trees were ancient, probably hundreds or thousands of years old. They were on three sides. The fourth side was Hammerhead Mountain.

He had just finished trimming the weeds at the edge of the cemetery when he heard the rumbling sound.

At first he couldn't place it, but it reminded him of faraway thunder, stopping and starting. It didn't even occur to him to look to the ground.

A few seconds passed, then he felt something at the bottom of his feet.

Shaking.

Cracking.

The ground opening up.

Three distinct lines of open earth appeared, one to his left, another to his right and a third coming towards him. The openings spread, causing headstones to crumble and fall into the ever-widening pits that were forming. Then he fell into a hole.

A coffin flew into the air. As it spun around, out came a body, actually a skeleton, draped with the stringy remnants of the clothes it was buried in. A mausoleum cracked, crumbled and virtually disintegrated, causing the four coffins inside to come flying out.

As parts of long-dead bodies and rotted wooden coffins and dirt and mud rained down upon him, Trevor managed to climb up to the top.

There was a ditch that seemed to be ten feet deep and another ten feet wide, a dozen or so coffins, some intact, some broken and bent, were spread out, as were a like number of corpses, probably brothers from the order, each in varying states of decomposition, some in the ground so long they were nothing but skeletons, others still maintaining a semblance of recognizable human form that suggested they'd only been dead a few years.

Trevor, himself a mess from the flying dirt and grass, tried to figure what he should do next. He was about to call his, boss, Brother David, when he saw something that shocked him.

Lying in the ground, partially buried, were two skeletons. They were huge. Trevor guessed that they were at least fifteen feet in height.

Giants?

It's a giant cemetery.

He couldn't take his eyes off of them. They were buried in what he guessed were two, twenty-five-foot-long graves each approximately ten feet deep and twenty feet wide. There was no coffin. The rotted remnants of burlap were wrapped around the body.

He would have to notify Brother David immediately.

"Trevor!" was all he heard as he turned and saw the sixty-something monk running towards him, out of breath.

He came to a stop at the edge of the giant's grave, stared into it, then looked at Trevor.

"Brother, these are the graves of giants."

"Yes. You know our secret."

"Giants?"

"Yes."

"It's amazing. Incredible!"

"This presents a problem for us."

"A problem?"

Suddenly, a voice he hadn't heard before spoke. "How trustworthy are you, Trevor?"

He turned around and saw a man he did not know, standing there. It was Abbot Gassner, the man in charge of St. Alban's.

He didn't know what to say. He didn't consider himself trustworthy at all, but he decided to lie. "Very, I guess."

The Abbot stared at him. "You must remain here."

"What?"

"You can't leave. Ever."

Trevor was stunned. "Why not?"

"You'll tell someone."

"It's just so amazing. I mean, why wouldn't you tell? It's incredible. I mean, *giants!*"

"We cannot tell."

"But... "

"I'm going to give you a choice, Trevor. You can stay with us or you can die."

Trevor stared into the deep-set brown eyes of the brother. He wasn't sure if he was kidding. He hadn't known him long enough to read the venom in his eyes.

"There will be no thinking about it. This is the choice you must make right now. Right this moment. Make your decision."

Trevor was shaking, perspiring. "What about my family? I live with mother. She's an invalid. I'm all she has. I can't leave her."

That was a lie. His mother had passed away when he was eleven and he hadn't seen his father since he abandoned the family fifteen years ago. His only

117

relative was an older brother with whom he lived sometimes."

"We'll handle your mother."

"She'll know I'm missing."

"She will be provided for."

"She'll call my cousin. They'll put out a search party."

Another lie. He had one cousin who lived in Michigan. They didn't speak.

"They won't find you in the reserve."

"Why would I be in the reserve?"

"It's where you will live. It's where you will spend the rest of your life."

The sentence made him shudder.

"I have a girlfriend. What about her?"

Another lie. He had a girl he slept with periodically for booty calls, but she was definitely not his girlfriend. He tried to engender sympathy.

"She'll be notified of your death."

"But I'm not dead."

"That's what your family will be told."

"But... "

"She'll get over you."

"Oh my God!"

"It will be a difficult life, but you will have a life. There are others there to keep you company. And there are the giants. They're friendly. They will be your friends, as well. It's unfortunate that you had to witness this. We will keep in communication with you, but your communication with the world will end. You won't have electricity. No radio or television or music or Internet. We'll provide you with books. All you want. In time you will adjust. You will."

"But... "

"Make your decision, Trevor. Right now. Stay or die."

Trevor hesitated for a few seconds, looked again at the giant bones in front him, then looked back at the monk. His heart was beating, his mind racing trying to take in the information.

"I want to live."

"Good. Now, we have to begin cleaning up this mess and we must eliminate every trace of the earthquake. We have much work today. Go over there and start picking up the bones."

"Yes, Abbot."

Trevor turned around. He didn't see Abbot Gassner nod to Brother David indicating for him to knock Trevor out. He felt something hit him in the head. He fell to the ground, unconscious.

He woke up on the other side of the fifty-foot ridge that blocked the entrance to the nature reserve.

Staring down at him was a fourteen-foot-tall giant, Richard, his wife, twelve-foot high, Aimee, and their four-year-old son, Damian, who stood just under five feet tall.

"Welcome," said Richard, grimly. "We won't hurt you, lad."

They talk? He sounds British.

Damian giggled, ran to Trevor and hugged him.

~~~~~~

It took almost six years before Trevor acknowledged to himself that he liked living in the reserve with the giants. In the outside world, he had no friends. He knew in his heart that no one would miss him.

Living in the reserve with the giants and the abnormals made him, for the first time in his life, feel needed. He felt responsible. He missed the creature comforts, but he was content in his role of leadership. And as Damian grew up, he came to view him as a kid brother.

He didn't want that to end, ever.

With Damian as his best friend and Juliet as his wife, life would be pleasant.

~~~~~~

By the time he got back to his cave, Trevor was hoping that the monks would not have heard about the crashed plane, but he was nervous. He knew enough about how things work when a plane goes down.

Someone will be looking for it. He wondered if they would have flight records that could pinpoint where a plane was when it lost communication, which meant they would know that the plane Juliet was on crashed in, or near, the reserve.

He was concerned that if Gassner learned about the crash and found out Trevor knew about it, and didn't tell him, there would be hell to pay.

But he knew that if he told Abbot Gassner that there was a survivor, the Abbot would be concerned that her family would be nosey. If he told them that there were no survivors, that they had all been incinerated in the crashed plane, that might make everything all right.

Tomorrow he would contact the Abbot, tell him about the plane crash from which there were no survivors and that would be it.

He wondered how long it would take Juliet to accept her fate. He remembered that it had taken him two years. He hoped it would be sooner for her because he was ready to court her.

If she liked him, in return, they could be together, a couple, and start a family. He couldn't get the image of the two of them walking through the forest holding hands out of his head.

She's beautiful. Perfect for me. I'm older, sure, but not that much older. And what other choice is there for her?

~~~~~~

In the bedroom, Juliet stared straight ahead, her thoughts concentrating on one thing: escape.

I've got to get out of here.

For the first time, she started to cry.

But how?

She heard her stomach growl. Damian had left her more fruit, but she wanted a burger, fries, onion rings and a salad.

She wished she could call her brother, and her father in Denver.

She tried to sleep, but kept going in and out.

Juliet heard the sounds of two men snoring loudly. She crept out of the room she was in and walked slowly to the entrance where she had come in. She peered outside into the darkness.

It was pitch black. There was no moonlight. She couldn't see anything except blackness.

The silence terrified her. She heard little noises. A branch crackling. A gust of wind. An odd sound from some kind of animal moving nearby. She wondered if there were monsters lurking. She tried to pinpoint the noises she heard.

Prehistoric sounds. That's what they are.

She remembered the line from *Game of Thrones*, which she was addicted to. 'The night is dark and full of terrors.'

The thought of having to stay in this place for the rest of her life made her feel crazy. She had to get out.

But how?

DAY

3

CHAPTER

15

Trevor tossed and turned all night trying to decide if he should tell the monks about the crashed plane. He would have to talk to Abbot Gassner, something he'd done periodically over the years.

Gassner ran the monastery, as well as the Smiling Monk jellies and jams business, with an iron hand. Trevor had become friendly with Brother Simon. They had never seen each other, but they'd spoken numerous times through the intercom the monks built for him.

He knew Gassner would want to know that there was a new normal-sized person living in the reserve. When he found out that it was a teenaged girl, Trevor wondered if it might give him pause to allow a rescue, which his predecessor had allowed one time. An infant and its mother had survived a crash near the only entrance to the reserve. The mother hadn't seen a giant or normal-sized person because she was unconscious. A monk had seen the plane she was in go in the trees. He went into the reserve, pulled her and her baby out of the fuselage and out of the reserve.

Then something dawned on him.

Juliet has seen the giants.

The Abbot would never let her go.

There was no reason to tell him about her.

I'll tell him that a plane crashed and all four people on it had died.

As he made his way to the locked entrance door where there was an intercom installed especially for him when he needed to contact the monks or they him, he was stopped by a giant foot.

He looked up and saw that it belonged to Martin, a giant he despised, who crouched down and smirked at him. "Victor told me about a girl in a crashed plane." His voice was raspy. He always reminded Trevor of the character Froggy the Gremlin with a cockney accent.

Trevor said nothing.

"Who is she with, Damian and Pete?"

"Yes."

"How old?"

"Young."

"How young?"

"Seventeen or eighteen."

"I need her to cook for my abnormals."

"No. I want her. She's mine."

Martin laughed. "Yours?"

"I need a partner. A wife."

"She's too young for you. Victor says she's a teenager."

"Damian found her."

"No. Victor was there first. Damian chased him away."

"What do you want, Martin?"

"Do the monks know about the girl?"

"No."

"Will you tell them?"

"I see no reason to."

"Then why are you here?"

"I need supplies."

Martin hesitated for several seconds. "I need her. My abnormals need her."

"I do too. She'll be the first female companion I've had since I got here."

Martin scratched his chin. "You were always nice to me, not like Pete and Damian. I have a solution. We can share her. Three-and-half days with us, three-and-half days with you. Fair enough, Trevor?"

He considered the idea. "Four with me, three with you. And I get her on Sundays."

Martin nodded. "You explain to the girl when the time is right. Does she have injuries from the crash?"

"Nothing that won't heal quickly."

"How many days?"

"Maybe a week."

"I'll make a place for her."

"I think we should wait awhile."

"Why? I need her now."

"She's difficult. I'll need more time to prepare her for life here."

Martin snorted. "Ten days. Then she comes with me."

Trevor nodded yes.

"What's her name?"

"Juliet."

"She pretty?"

"Yes."

"How tall?"

"I don't know for sure. Maybe five feet five."

"Too bad. If she was ten more feet, I could have her."

Martin smirked and lumbered away.

Trevor kept on toward the entrance where the intercom was. He picked it up, punched in three numbers and waited.

Brother George answered after four rings.

"Yes, Trevor?"

"We have a problem, George. I need to talk to Abbot Gassner. It's an emergency. A plane has crashed in the reserve."

"When? I didn't hear or see any plane go down."

"Two days ago. No survivors. The wreckage has been buried. No one will ever find it."

"Are you sure, Trevor?"

"Yes. I saw where it was hidden. Six-four-seven found the plane hanging in a tree."

"And you're positive it can't be found?"

"Yes. Will you tell the Abbot or should I?"

"You do it. He'll want to hear all the details. I'll put you right through. Hang on."

Brother George immediately patched in the call to Abbot Gassner. Within thirty seconds he was on the line.

"Yes, Trevor. What's so urgent?"

"There's been a plane crash in the reserve."

Gassner sat up. "How many were on board?"

"Three plus the pilot. The plane is buried in Jawbone ravine. It will never be found. I thought you should know in case you get any calls from the airport."

"Thank you, Trevor. When did it happen?"

"Probably the day before. Number six-forty-seven stumbled on it. He said there was minimal smoke that might have drifted upward, but he stopped it pretty fast."

"There's been nothing on the news."

"It was a small, single engine plane. Maybe it'll be harder to keep track of."

"Flight plans can be checked. I'm certain the National Safety Review Board will know that it went down in or near the reserve. Are you *sure* the plane wreckage is out of sight?"

"Yes. I checked it myself. It will never be found."

"I'll try to keep them out. Thank you for letting me know about this. Do you need any other supplies?"

"The usual will do." Trevor had learned to never miss an opportunity to get provisions. "And I could use a new shirt and pair of jeans." He thought about asking for woman's underwear, but thought better of it. "And some underwear and socks."

"Fine. We'll get them to you tomorrow morning."

"Thank you, Abbot."

They both hung up.

Trevor hoped he made the right decision. He was trying to accomplish two things: protect Juliet's life and pave the way for a relationship with her. He knew it was selfish of him to be acting so fast with her, but the loneliness he'd experienced over the last twelve years was unbearable. He needed human contact. He needed to be loved by a woman and if she wouldn't love him, he would love her enough for the both of them.

And he needed sex.

While he waited, Trevor pondered the situation. Even though people had died, Juliet's arrival had gotten his adrenaline pumping, something that hadn't happened in years. That he would have to share her with Martin wasn't so bad. He wanted her for a good thing. And it was true that all of his abnormals were getting old and senile.

He really did need Juliet's help.

On top of that, there were only a handful of giants left and save for Damian, the others were all up in years, giant years, which meant they would be dying off. Soon.

Trevor always feared the day that Damian would be the last giant because he knew he might try to escape, even if he would die in the process.

Without Damian, he would be totally alone with no one to talk to. He wouldn't be able to live in a situation like that. Why would the monks continue to keep him prisoner if there were no giants to protect?

But now, with Juliet, he would have a companion and maybe, if he were lucky, a lover.

Or a wife.

And children.

Trevor loved children.

As for Abbot Gassner, he felt calmer after talking with Trevor. In his twenty-eight years of being in charge, he'd been warned by The Vatican of the importance of keeping people out of the reserve. This plane crash was the latest in close calls.

Thank God they all died.

But the closest of calls came from the normal-sized people trying to get *out* of the reserve, people who tried to escape. Then, he had to involve Albert Sulpience, the Knight Templar he called when someone made an attempt. It had happened three times in his tenure and three times Sulpience had to be contacted.

Albert Sulpience was a man of many colors and shadings. Besides being a member of The Grand Commandery of Knights Templar and based in New York City, he was also a lecturer at Columbia University on medieval history and had Above Top-Secret Clearance in the Department of Defense, where he retained the rank of Major. He had a special interest on behalf of The Roman Catholic Church: giants. He was their primary enforcer.

Most of the sightings and the random news items occurred in Europe or Asia, but he was always the spokesman for the Church in North America.

He was a descendant of eleven generations of Knights Templar. When his time came to be initiated into the organization it was the penultimate day of his life. He was twenty-eight years old. Now, twenty-one years later, he was as devoted an advocate as his first day.

The Poor Fellow-Soldiers of Christ and of the Temple of Solomon, commonly known as the Knights Templar, the Order of the Temple or simply as Templars, were among the wealthiest and powerful of the Western Christian military orders, and were among the most prominent actors of the Christian finance. The organization existed for nearly two centuries during the Middle Ages.

Officially endorsed by the Catholic Church around 1129, the Order became a favored charity throughout Christendom and grew rapidly in membership and power. Templar knights, in their distinctive white mantles with a red cross, were among the most skilled fighting units of the Crusades. Non-combatant members of the Order managed a large economic infrastructure throughout Christendom, innovating financial techniques that were an early form of banking and building fortifications across Europe and the Holy Land.

The Templars' existence was tied closely to the Crusades. When the Holy Land was lost, support for the Order faded. Rumors about the Templars' secret initiation ceremony created mistrust and King Philip IV of France, deeply in debt to the Order, took advantage of the situation. In 1307, many of the Order's members in France were arrested, tortured into giving false confessions, and then burned at the stake. Under pressure from King Philip, Pope Clement V disbanded the Order in 1312. The abrupt disappearance of a major part of the European infrastructure gave rise to speculation and legends, which have kept the "Templar" name alive into the modern day.

But the Templars still existed under secrecy. They consist of smaller numbers, and they still protect the Church. Nowadays they use state of the art technology and equipment to do their work.

Sulpience, like all Templars, was trained to be ready on a second's notice when the Catholic Church called, not that the call came that often. For him, possibly three or four times a year. In the current year, he hadn't been contacted once. It was mid-July, but if the call did come, he would be ready to go.

Abbot Gassner sighed deeply. He felt oddly relaxed.

Thank the Lord I didn't have to call Sulpience.

CHAPTER

16

Juliet lay on the bed unable to get comfortable. Her head hurt less and she felt rested. She wished she could luxuriate in a hot bubble bath with her favorite oils and lotions. Her hair felt dirty. She wondered if they had shampoo in this place, but she knew they didn't.

At least I'm okay.

She noticed a pail of water and a rag that was meant to be a towel. She assumed it was there for her to wash. She noticed the fresh pair of jeans and shirt on the table next to her.

As she gave herself a sponge bath and changed clothes, her thoughts were all over the place, racing a mile a minute. How could this have happened to her? She was six weeks away from starting college. She had so many things she wanted to do, and now she finds out she's in the cave of a giant, being held captive by some monks and worst of all, she's being told she'll have to stay here forever.

She tried to relive the crash, but it was difficult as she'd been asleep for most of the flight. She remembered hearing Georgette and Luc scream. The shock of the plane spiraling down woke her up. She recalled the pilot was warning her to prepare for a crash, and the next thing she remembered was seeing the giant.

She thought about her brother and father. The idea of never seeing them again was unbearable. To lose her mother the year before and now, to lose the rest of her family? It was too much to comprehend.

She decided to stand up to see if she could walk.

With a little pressure from her left arm, she got out of the gigantic bed. She felt a bit dizzy at first, but after ten steps she had completely regained her balance. She walked back and forth across the room.

She felt strong. She made her way to the door, opened it and walked toward the lantern light, which emanated from a far corner. She stepped outside and breathed in the fresh air.

It was a sunny day, but chilly. She heard birds chirping. She couldn't get used to the huge trees, some reaching hundreds of feet into the sky and their trunks appeared to be thirty or forty feet around. The grass on the ground was a vibrant green with the residue of rain. It was interrupted by a worn path, fifteen feet wide.

The path must be so wide to accommodate the giants.

She decided to stay on the path as she kept walking, slowly at first, but with each step she felt stronger. She felt her muscles loosening. She continued breathing in the fresh air. She figured she had walked about two hundred yards away from Damian's cave. She had no idea where she was or which way was north, south, east or west, but she didn't care. She was just happy to be alive and walking.

She kept moving, trying to gather her thoughts about her predicament. She missed her iPhone, her iPad, her friends, her brother, her father, food, everything.

Then she heard something.

Movement.

She turned toward the noise and saw a snake of some kind staring at her. She froze. It was about six feet long.

Oh my God!

She hated snakes.

She wasn't sure what to do. Should she stay there or try to run.

Suddenly, the snake slithered away.

Now I have to worry about snakes.

She kept on walking, following the path, secretly hoping it would lead her to a way out, but she knew in her heart that wouldn't happen.

Suddenly the path veered off into three smaller paths. Which one to take? She decided to stay with the one she was on, but it turned into a hill, which she followed, and then there was another hill.

She kept walking, going up, then down, moving right, then left. She came to the river she'd seen the day before. She wondered where it came from and where it led. The water looked pure enough to drink, but she was hesitant. She decided to walk along the riverbank with the hope that she would find out where it started.

After half an hour or was it an hour, she observed that the river seemed to be going nowhere. Then she realized something that horrified her.

She was lost.

She turned to her left, then her right trying to get a sense of where she was. She had no idea. She turned around and tried to figure out where she had come from, but she hadn't been watching the path she was on and there was no path any longer. There was just five-foot high foliage, leaves, rocks and fallen branches.

When she started to move again, she heard identical movement. She would stop, and so would whatever was following her, but an ever-present growling hung in the air.

Her heart started beating rapidly, twice as hard and fast as normal. She wanted to call out Damian's name, but was afraid the noise might irritate whatever was following her or attract another animal or the giant she had seen in the plane.

She decided to keep walking the way she had come from, but after thirty yards she felt confused. Nothing looked the same. Not that she had been paying attention. There was nothing except trees, trees and more trees.

She wanted to run, but her leg hurt and she still felt weak. She had no idea how to get back to Damian's cave. She got the idea of looking for her footprints and following them, but there were none. She was getting even more frightened.

What if Damian can't find me?

Then she heard a loud, clumsy noise, as if something was moving towards her. She turned around and saw Victor running towards her. He was yelling "Youuuuu mmmmminnnnneee!" He leaned over and grabbed her, but roughly, not gentlemanly like Damian. And he kept her ensnared in his hand, unlike Damian who put her gently on his shoulder. She felt like a rabbit that he had caught and was dragging her to his cave. She screamed the only thing she could think of.

"Damian!!!"

Victor kept running, but he wasn't as fast or as young as Damian. He gradually went from a run to a slow lumber, but Juliet continued to scream for Damian.

Suddenly, Victor stopped cold.

Then she saw a familiar face. The woman she'd seen the day before.

Gretchen.

And with her were two other women, both thin, gray-haired, haggard, pale, wrinkled and old. She recognized one as the woman she saw with Gretchen the day Damian rescued her.

"Victor!" she stated with authority as if she were a school principal. "Put that girl down." Victor just stared at her. "Put her down right now!"

"Damian steal her from me."

"She is not an object," said Gretchen. "She is a person. Put her down."

Victor did so. The instant he let her go she moved quickly to Gretchen and stood behind her, almost as if she were a child.

"Apologize to her."

Victor glanced down at Juliet. "I sorry."

"Now go back to your territory."

"It not fair. We need a bloody cook."

"We all need something," said the mean-faced woman next to Gretchen. "You alright, honey?"

"Yes, thank you."

"You shouldn't be out by yourself," the mean-faced woman said.

Victor shook his head back and forth, then walked off.

"Juliet," said Gretchen. "Margo is right. What are you doing out here alone?"

"I went for a walk and he grabbed me."

"That was stupid," said the mean-faced woman, shaking her head back and forth. "Just dumb."

"It's always best to have company around here," said Gretchen." She turned to the other women. "This is the young girl I told you about."

"I figured that out," snapped the mean-faced woman shaking her head back and forth.

"Juliet, I'd like you to meet Barbara and Margo."

Margo, the mean-faced one, nodded her head as she looked Juliet over. Barbara smiled and said a soft, "Hello" without enthusiasm.

"Don't go out by yourself 'til you get your bearings," said Margo. "You're just askin' for trouble." Juliet noticed a New England accent.

"That's enough, Margo," said Gretchen.

"I didn't realize how far I walked," said Juliet.

"Make sure you learn your lesson because we may not be here to save you next time," Margo chimed in for good measure.

"She's been here for one day, Margo. Please stop."

"Just doin' it for her own good."

"This is where we live," said Gretchen. "We have plenty of room. You'll be staying with us when you're healthy. Damian told me. When you come, we'll help you get settled in."

That is not gonna happen.

"How'd you get into this hateful, wretched place?" asked Margo.

"Plane crash. I was the only survivor."

"Too bad."

Is she saying too bad because I survived or because I didn't?

"Margo, you're being very rude."

"It's the truth. I wish I woulda died when I got here." She glared at Juliet. "You will to."

"Why?" asked Gretchen.

"Because every day I'm here has been like bein' in hell. I lost my husband, my cats, my house, my *life!*" She turned to Gretchen and Barbara. "I'm goin' back. You comin'?"

Barbara nodded yes, smiled at Juliet and walked off with Margo.

"Would you like to come with us to see where you'll be living?" asked Gretchen.

The idea of seeing their cave frightened and disgusted Juliet.

"I can't. I have to be getting back."

"Do you know the way?"

"Not really."

"Then I'll walk you there," said Gretchen.

"Thank you."

Normally, Juliet walked at a brisk pace, but because her leg still hurt, she didn't mind moving slowly.

"Do you and Barbara feel the way Margo does about being in this place?"

"Barbara doesn't talk much. We think she has some form of Alzheimer's. It started about nine years ago. She has no medication. It's difficult. We look after her."

"I'm so sorry."

"Where are you from?" asked Gretchen.

"Denver."

"I'm from New Hampshire. We have so much to talk about. Who did you leave behind?"

The question upset Juliet. "Uh, my dad and my brother."

"What about your mother?"

"She died last year."

"I left behind three sons. Fourteen, sixteen and nineteen. And my husband."

"I'm sorry."

"They're all grown men now," said Gretchen. "I think about them every day. My husband has probably remarried by now. You're lucky you don't have children. Leaving them alone was the hardest part. You never stop worrying about them. It'll be hard for you at the beginning, Juliet, but in time you'll get used to it. You really will. Do you have a boyfriend?"

The question surprised Juliet. "No. I'm going to college in six weeks and I didn't have time."

"You won't be going to college, dear," said Gretchen gently.

Juliet remained silent for a few seconds.

"You know that, don't you, Juliet?"

"Damian keeps telling me that this place is escape-proof, but there must be a way."

"There isn't. You're lucky you didn't have a boyfriend. Margo told me she and her husband used to fight all the time, but she loved him. Not seeing him took years to get used to. My sister Linda and I didn't get along, but I loved her. You miss the people you aren't even close with. Margo is still as bitter about being here as the day she arrived."

"Didn't you ever try to escape?"

Gretchen smiled wryly and laughed. "Of course. Everyone did. In fact, Margo was the most aggressive of us all. She's very emotional, a bit of a hothead. It took her years to accept that she was never going home. You're young. I don't know how much time you'll need. You'll want to escape. You're probably thinking about it already, but it won't happen. You'll spend a long time looking for ways, as I did, as everyone did, but there is no way out. Margo gave up after five years, I'd say. Be patient with her. Deep down she's nice."

Juliet processed the information and it made her sick. She felt the dry heaves coming again.

"Oh-Oh," said Gretchen.

"What?" asked Juliet.

"We have company."

Then Juliet saw the giant foot, and another one, and two more. Victor was back with another giant. She froze in her tracks.

She got a clearer look at Victor this time. She guessed he was in his late twenties, the other in his early thirties. They weren't handsome and physically fit like Damian. Victor was grossly fat with a huge stomach and long, hanging jowls, which he was scratching. She noticed drool dripping from his mouth. The handful of teeth he had left was yellowed.

The other one had a goofy expression on his face, almost as if he'd had a stroke and never properly healed. He reminded her of the stoners who went to her high school: dull, deadened eyes and undeveloped personalities.

They moved toward Juliet and Gretchen, surrounding them. The giant with the goofy expression moved closer to Juliet.

"Let me do the talking," said Gretchen. "I've dealt with these idiots before." She turned to Victor. "You know you're not supposed to be here, Victor. I just reprimanded you and I don't want to do it again. You have to listen."

"We need girl real bad," the other giant said firmly. He crouched down and stared at Juliet. He smelled like a wild animal, his breath made her nauseous, he was filthy and looked like he hadn't bathed in a month. Or a year. "You *ours*!"

"She's nobody's!" said Gretchen.

"She come with us," said Victor. He reached for her with his right hand.

She jumped backward and he reached for her again, this time his huge fingers nipping at her shirt.

Then she heard Damian's voice.

"Leave her alone, Huey."

Huey? The other one's name is Huey? How did they get these names?

Damian stepped in between the giants and Juliet.

"I told you that I'd be talking about her with Martin when she's healthy."

"She look healthy to me," said Victor.

"You're not supposed to be here. You know that."

"You come our territory. We come yours."

"Yeah," said Huey.

"I wanted Huey to see her," said Victor.

"Okay. He's seen her. Now go."

"After you talk to Martin we be back."

"Fine. Go."

"We need a woman real bad."

"I know that," said Damian. "Martin and I will work it out. Go."

The giants glared at Damian, then at Juliet, then at Gretchen, then turned and walked away without looking back.

"I told you that it was dangerous for you," said Damian.

"I just needed to stretch," said Juliet. "So, that's twice you rescued me."

"Damian is very good at rescuing us," said Gretchen with a smile. "Aren't you, dear?"

"I do my best."

"Juliet, when you're ready, you can stay with me, if you like."

I'll never be ready.

Juliet didn't want to cause a scene so she played along.

"Thank you."

"I want to ask you about what's happening in the world, but let's leave that for another time. I'll go for now, but if you have any questions don't hesitate to ask. I'll be more than happy to help with your transition." She smiled.

I'm not transitioning anywhere.

"Okay."

"Whenever you're ready."

Gretchen winked at Damian and left.

"How long has she been here?" asked Juliet.

"Probably twenty-five years, maybe longer."

Oh my God. I am not gonna be here in twenty-five years.

"Let's go back." He extended his left hand, which was her cue to jump on it. He whooshed her up to his shoulder like he did before.

"Can we not go back? I'm feeling claustrophobic. I need to take a bath. I know you don't have a shower."

"We have a waterfall you can use."

"That would be great."

He reached for her and placed her on his shoulder.

"Ready?"

"Yes," said Juliet. "Can you not run? I can't really see anything when we move fast."

"Okay. Running tires me out. The more I run the better I sleep at night."

After she got a good grip he started walking. As she clung to Damian's collar Juliet felt safe.

She shut her eyes.

"How did it feel to walk in the forest?" Damian asked.

"My leg hurt a little at first, but I can move almost in a normal way."

"That's good."

He moved at a good pace, but noticeably slower.

"What's it like to be a giant?" Juliet said.

Damian chuckled. "Nobody ever asked me that before."

"It must be amazing to be so much taller than everybody else?"

"It's strange. I don't feel taller. Sometimes I feel smaller than everyone, even the abnormals."

What he said shocked Juliet. "I don't understand. I would've thought that being so big made you feel like a Greek god?" She hesitated for a second. "Do you know about Greek gods?"

"Yes. Trevor taught me. Zeus. Neptune. I never felt like a god. Not for one second. I have a question for you, Juliet. What's it like out there?"

"Out there?"

"Being free? Trevor told me, but I'd like to hear it from you."

She'd never even considered the idea of being free. She'd taken it for granted.

"Amazing" was the only thing she could think of to say.

Damian considered the remark. "I feel that way when I run."

"That's the pheromones in your brain. They help to clear your head. It's a chemical reaction. I like to run too."

Damian smiled at her.

"I swim too," he said.

"In what? Is there a lake or something?"

"Yes. It's where I get water. Once you settle in, I can take you there. Nobody uses it to swim except me. The other giants can't do it. They're afraid of the water. Trevor taught me."

Once I settle in?

I will not be settling in. God please don't let me settle in.

"You'll be living close by. I can pick you up and we can swim. I can show you around, tell you which places to avoid. "

"What would I need to avoid?"

"Remote places in other sections," said Damian. "Falling trees. Swamps. You should stay in this area. Do you know how to fish?"

"No."

"I'll teach you. I assume you don't know how to farm?"

"No. Why?"

"Mainly we eat fish and vegetables. More than anything, we're farmers. Gretchen and the other women all pitch in."

"You said I'd be living with the normal-sized people."

"You'll be living with Gretchen and the other women."

I can't live with old women. I need my space. I need my stuff.

"Why can't I live near you?"

"I told you. Because of the difference in our sizes, it could be dangerous. Once you settle in, you'll adapt."

"I don't want to settle in, Damian. I want to get out of here. I'd rather die than be stuck here forever."

The statement stunned Damian. "Die? You would really rather die?"

"Yes. I can tell you right now I'm gonna be a runner. I don't know where I'm gonna run to or how I'll do it, but I can't stay here. I can't. I'll try to run every day I'm here. I will never stop trying."

Damian didn't know what to say. Juliet started up again.

"What I can't wrap my head around is that the monks won't let anyone leave?" said Juliet.

"If they let you go, they know you'll tell," said Damian.

"Tell *what*?"

"About me. About my uncle. That giants exist. That giants are real and have always existed."

"Why would they care? It would change the way we look at things, certainly at religion."

"Yes. That's the problem. What will that do to the religions of the world?"

"But you can talk. You can think. And you're intelligent. And your British accent. I am still speechless about that."

"Their orders have always come from Rome. The Vatican wants our existence kept secret. I think I know why?"

Juliet waited for his answer.

"This is some of the oral history my mother told me. There was once a race of giants in Europe. They lived peacefully in remote sections of countries. They kept to themselves. There was some kind of natural disaster that killed most of them off. The ones who were left took to the hills and the mountains to get away from the disease. Some made their way to Africa. They bothered no one for centuries. At some point in time, during the fifteenth century, a giant was spotted wandering aimlessly near civilization in Italy. He was sick. They captured him. Brought him to Rome, to The Vatican. Christianity was a fact. The leaders of the Church decided that the world couldn't know that giants existed. That's when the scourge began. Because of our size, we didn't fit the model of what good Christians should look like. How would you explain thirteen-to-twenty-foot beings on God's earth? The race died out, except for a handful here and there. They managed to find most of us and keep us in hiding until we died off."

He held out his right hand displaying the ring his mother had given him. Juliet stared at it and decided it was pure gold lined with rubies.

"My mother gave me this. She said it's been passed down for centuries. She said it came from Mont Blanc in France where the giants still remain. She told me that this ring makes me a leader and that if I got to Mont Blanc, I would not only be with my ancestors, but I would lead them."

"Lead them in what?"

"She said I would know when I got there." He stopped. "Here we are. See it?"

Juliet looked up at the waterfall and smiled. It was the first time she'd done so since she got here.

It struck her as being about thirty-feet wide. As she studied it, she wondered where the water was coming from.

"It's so beautiful. I don't understand much about these things, but where does it come from?"

"A river that winds its way around Hammerhead Mountain. If you're wondering about escaping by following the river, don't bother. No one really knows where the water begins and ends. It just comes. You can get undressed and stand under the waterfall. I'll keep watch."

"Okay."

"And I won't look at you."

"Thank you."

Juliet removed her clothes and walked into the waterfall. She'd always wanted to do this. She'd seen at least a dozen movies where people, usually young lovers, took romantic showers under the waterfall.

The water was incredibly cold, almost icy, but she didn't care. She got accustomed to it within thirty seconds. She closed her eyes and remembered taking showers at home. Even though she knew she wasn't dreaming being here, with her eyelids shut, she could escape the horror that she was experiencing.

She wished she had a bar of soap and shampoo and conditioner and moisturizer and skin cream and lotion and toothpaste and mouth wash and everything she took for granted.

Across the lake, hidden behind a tree, stood Trevor, watching her.

CHAPTER

17

Following Edward Purdell's instructions, Greg Pine caught a plane out of LaGuardia Airport first thing that morning to the Plattsburg Airport. He bought a round trip ticket with the Master Card his father had lent him for the trip to New York in case of an emergency. He knew that what happened to Juliet was a major emergency, but he still hadn't called his dad to tell him. On three separate occasions he grabbed his phone to do it, but thought better of it. His dad could do nothing, so better that he didn't know that Juliet's plane was missing.

Edward and Teddy met him and took him immediately to Teddy's single engine touring plane, which he kept at the airport.

"Didn't think you were so young," said Edward.

Greg shrugged. "My sister's seventeen. I'm sixteen."

Despite the fact that it was illegal, the plan was for Teddy Germaine to fly over Cassoulet Reserve several times. The hope was that maybe they would spot a crashed plane in the trees.

"We'll look for signs of a plane crash," said Teddy. "but I want to warn you, the forest is dense. There are some sections where there are no trees, but if her plane went down it would require luck to spot it. All we'll be able to see, if we're lucky, is a glimpse of silver or white or whatever color the plane is. If we can spot it there's hope."

"What if we can't?" asked Greg.

"Hard to say. Either it went down in the reserve or it didn't. We'll be able to see it or we won't."

Edward wanted to add one more possibility to Teddy's list: that the giants living in the reserve might have buried it, but knew now was not the time.

As Edward listened to Teddy talk, he ruminated over the bad news he'd been given by Juliet's brother. He'd called his contacts at the airport and found out that the Cessna was indeed missing, but that they still had no idea where it had gone off the radar. There would be no search for the plane, at least not yet.

In the event he was caught, Teddy had already come up with an excuse for why he was flying in a no-fly zone.

"My asthma took hold of me," he would say. "I couldn't breathe then I couldn't find my inhaler. It was horrible."

He was confident the lie would work if he had to use it.

For the next half-hour the plane cruised over the reserve, narrowly approaching the treetops. All three looked, but saw nothing. Edward used a pair of high-powered binoculars. No plane had crashed. Or if one did, the giants had hidden or buried it. Edward and Teddy felt sad both for Greg Pine and themselves. They both needed an excuse to get into the reserve. Spotting Juliet's plane would have been perfect because they could lead the National Safety Review Board to it.

"There's nothing," said Edward, his tone forlorn.

~~~~~~

Juliet heard the plane during its first pass over the reserve, but she couldn't see it. She was inside Damian's cave with him and Trevor. Excited, she ran outside and looked up, hoping the plane would come by again. She screamed, "Down here! I'm down here!" again and again, but they couldn't hear or see her. The trees blocked her from sight. Every time it flew by, she screamed until her throat ached. She fell to the ground, sobbing.

Damian and Trevor didn't try to stop her. They knew she was too far away to be heard or seen.

~~~~~~

"What am I supposed to do now?" Greg asked.

"The National Safety Review board has announced that the plane is missing, but they haven't announced any plans for a search."

"Can't I go to a newspaper or a TV station?"

"On the news it said that there were two other kids and the pilot. Maybe, if you could get together with their parents, or if the pilot had a family..."

"How do I do that?" Greg said, frustrated.

Edward felt for the kid, but he didn't know what to tell him. "Just wait. Just wait."

"I feel so helpless," said Greg. "I need to do something, but I don't know what." He wanted to call his dad.

Hearing the boy's angst, Edward decided to take a risk and tell him about the giants. But first he had to tell him more about the monks.

"Greg, I hesitated to tell you this in our earlier conversation, but now might be the right time. You need to know about the monks. They come across as very friendly and kind, and frankly, they are. But when it comes to gaining entrance to the reserve, they get strange. They basically control the reserve."

After Greg listened to Edward explain the restricted area, he had one response

"If they know a plane has crashed in their part of the reserve, they would do nothing about it?"

"Yes," said Edward. "And there's not a damn thing you can do about it either."

Greg sat back in his chair, uncomfortable. "Why not?"

"Because they're job is to protect something."

"Protect what?"

Edward got a serious look on his face. "Please don't think I'm crazy."

"Tell me." He remembered what the clerk at his hotel had said about Edward Purdell.

"Some say that it's giants."

"Giants?" Greg arched his eyebrows suspiciously. "Whattya mean 'giants'?"

Purdell reached into his satchel and pulled out a scrapbook. He placed it in front of Greg.

"Have a look."

Greg leafed through it. He found page after page of photocopied articles, some short, some long, about giants, their bones being discovered and theories on their existence. There were dozens of photographs of large skeletons, some real, some fake and mixed in among the articles were other pieces debunking the sightings. Had he taken the time to read them, he would've noticed that one name kept popping up in many of the debunking pieces: Albert Sulpience.

As Greg leafed through the material, Purdell tried to figure out what the kid was thinking. He didn't look bored, but he also didn't look captivated. Edward had learned not to push it with the people he'd brought up the giants to. Most of them thought he was out of his mind.

"What I'm trying to tell you, Greg, is that there are giants living in the reserve and the monks are keeping them there."

"Giants," Greg said, deadpan, shaking his head. He felt that he was the adult.

"Yes. If your sister's plane went down and, if she survived, she might be there."

"With the giants?"

"Yes."

Greg stared at him. "Will they hurt her?"

"I can't say. If we can get into the eastern section of the reserve, I can find them. What I've wanted to do for most of my life is find a real, live giant and present him to the world. I know that they exist because I've seen one."

"I have too," said Teddy. "I saw a face and a hand when I was flying over the reserve."

"I saw a full skeleton," said Edward.

"Why didn't you tell the police or somebody?" asked Greg.

"It disintegrated before my eyes. A pile of dust wouldn't cut it."

Greg turned to Teddy. "Why didn't you tell what you saw?"

"I did, but without proof, they thought I was lying or drunk. We need real, hardcore evidence."

"If Teddy and I can get into the eastern section of the reserve, we can find the giants and your sister," said Edward. "If she's still alive."

Greg had heard enough. He thought that Edward and Teddy were out of their minds.

"Would you take me back to the airport?" asked Greg. "I want to get out of this place."

"Yes, of course." Edward realized it was best to leave it alone.

CHAPTER

18

Trevor had spent the previous night figuring out what to say to Juliet. He'd sensed that she wasn't very warm toward him, so to have him suggest that she come and live with his people would be a mistake. He had to broach the subject of her spending half her time with Martin's abnormals. It would be a lot for her to handle.

He knew he would have to be less preachy with her. He would need to give her space and time to absorb that she would never be leaving or see her family and friends again. He knew it took him a long time to accept his own loss and he assumed she would be the same.

This time he was pleasant and friendly.

Juliet was too.

He began by telling her the rules.

"It's summer now. You'll see that it's the best time of year. Better than spring which is also nice, but chilly, and better than fall which is less nice because it rains all the time. The winds from the Adirondacks start to come in from the south and even stronger winds come from Canada. The winter is the hardest because of the freezing temperature and the snow. We stay in our caves for much of each day. There is no heat except for the warmth that comes from the fires we make. When I say that we live together I mean that we do it for companionship. Each of us has our own dwelling, but we still have to be watchful. We each have a job. I'm the youngest, so I have most of the responsibilities. I'm glad about that. Why? It keeps me busy. If I'm busy, at the end of each day I'm tired and I will sleep. When I wake up the next day, it is just like the day before and the day before that. The only times that I spend my days differently is in the winter. I try to keep warm. I hunt for game. I fish. We have a communal kitchen. One of the older women did the cooking, but she got sick. If you can cook, maybe that will be your job. You will also have to work in the fields with the crops."

Work in the fields?

"I don't know a thing about cooking," Juliet said.

"We'll teach you." He changed the subject. "Obviously, the giants are big and we're small.

No shit.

"We can't live together with them because they might accidentally step on us and crush us to death."

"I already know that. Damian told me."

"Okay. When I first came here twelve years ago there were nineteen normal-sized people. Ten have died. I don't spend much time with them because of the age difference, but I look after them. Once you're okay, we can move you to our quarters."

"I have to live with *you*?"

"No. Near me. Next door to me, so to speak."

She looked at him with skepticism. "In a cave."

"I'll help you make it comfortable."

"Where do I go to the bathroom?"

"Outside. In an outhouse."

Oh my God!

"I have to do my business outside?"

Trevor nodded.

"How do I wash?"

"We have water. You'll take sponge baths or you can go to the waterfall when the weather is warm."

"Are there mirrors?"

"Yes."

"What will I do all day and at night?"

Trevor hesitated for several seconds, then said, "Survive."

She said nothing.

"That's all we do here," said Trevor. "Survive. Once you get used to it, you'll grow comfortable with it. You'll be a cook."

Like hell I will.

"I don't feel well," said Juliet. "I'd like to be alone. I think I'd like to try and rest."

"Okay," said Trevor.

He nodded for Damian to come with him. Damian glanced at Juliet and made eye contact, then followed Trevor out.

When they were outside of the room where Juliet was, Trevor said, "She hates me, doesn't she?"

"I don't know."

"Everything I say comes out wrong. I have to start bringing her good news."

"Like what?"

Trevor said nothing. "Maybe I should leave her alone for a few days."

"Not a bad idea. Telling her that she'll have to stay here for the rest of her life and that she'll never see anyone she cares about again? That she'll never have one normal second in her entire life?"

"She has to accept those things, Damian, like I did. Like all of us did."

"Let me talk to her, Trevor."

"What will you say?"

"I don't know. I think she trusts me. I'll talk to her. Give her some space."

"Alright, Damian. And you'll talk to her about me?"

"Yes."

"Okay, then."

Trevor left.

Damian went into the room where Juliet was.

"He's gone," said Damian.

"Good. He makes my skin crawl. For as long as I'm living here, I don't want to be anywhere near him."

They were silent for a couple of minutes until Juliet spoke. "Before you told me that you were the youngest giant."

"Yes."

"There are no young female giants, right?"

"Not here."

"What do you mean?"

"There are some in Mont Blanc in France."

"But Trevor said that all the giants left in the world are here."

"That's his opinion. My mother would never lie. People who love you don't lie to you."

"Even if she was right, France is so far away," said Juliet. "There would be no way for you to get there. And before you can even think about that, you have to get out of here."

"I know that, but I didn't have a way out." Damian took a deep breath and sighed deeply. "Until you came."

"Me?"

"I've wanted to leave since I was thirteen, since my mother gave me the ring, but I couldn't because I'd get caught, and who knows what the scientists would do to me."

165

"Even if you could get out and live free for one day, it would be better than living here for the rest of your life."

The remark resonated with him. Damian looked away. He knew that she was right.

He decided to tell her his secret.

"What if I told you there is a way out?"

She stared at him in shock.

What is he telling me?

"What?" she asked. "Is there?"

"With your help I can set you free."

With my help?

"What can I do?"

"I found a way out, but I can only do it with someone your size."

"I thought you said it was impossible."

"There is a way. A passage opened up on the mountain."

Oh my God!

"I'll do whatever you want."

"Can you drive a truck?"

CHAPTER

19

"**S**tick shift or automatic?" asked Juliet.

Please be automatic.

"I don't know."

"Because I never learned stick shift," she said. "And I've never driven a truck. What kind is it?"

Damian sighed. "I don't know. Big enough that I could fit in it."

"Then it's big. Oh my God! I don't think I can drive one of those. I hope it's not stick. They're scary and complicated with their hydraulic brakes and multiple gearshifts. So, let's say it's something I can manage. Where are you gonna find this truck?"

"I told you the monks have a factory."

"Smiling Monk jams?" said Juliet.

"They keep the manufacturing plant separate from the retreat house. There are a dozen trucks that go in and out every day. They come in empty at the end of each day, then every morning they're filled up. With you driving and me hiding inside, I would be safe."

"Are you sure you can fit inside?"

"I measured it."

"How did you do that?"

"I climbed down the mountain," he said.

What?

"When?"

"Three times."

He went down? He got out and he came back? Of course he came back. Where would he go?

"At night. I went to where the trucks are parked. The rear storage area is about twenty feet long. I can sit in it, and it's wide enough for me to lay inside if I want to curl up."

"Was it hard for you to come back?"

"No. I was afraid. I needed to make a plan. I had to have somebody to drive the truck. Until you got here that was impossible so I never thought about it. And then you came and I hoped you'd be a runner and..."

"Where do you want me to drive you?"

"To Mont Blanc."

Is he crazy?

"You can't get to France in a truck, Damian. You have to fly or be on a ship. You need another plan."

Damian frowned. "It's the only place I can go."

"I hate to be negative, but you can't get there, Damian."

"But... "

"You know how you keep telling me that there's no way out of here? There is definitely no way for you to get to France."

"I found a way out of here. Maybe there's a way to get there."

"There isn't. I have a better plan. You need to go public."

"No."

"If you can really get us out of here, if we're lucky, we'll get to New York City," she said. "Once we're there, we'll tell the world and you'll be free."

"Trevor says they'll turn me into a guinea pig, keep me prisoner and probably kill me."

"Trevor's wrong. They're not going to kill you. Once they realize you can talk and that you're educated and intelligent, you'll get your own talk show."

"What's that?"

"Never mind for now. If I can't drive this truck, and I'm pretty certain I can't, we need somebody else to drive it, otherwise we won't be going anywhere."

Damian stared at her, looking bereft.

"Then we'll have to climb back up," he said dejectedly.

"Couldn't I stay down?" she asked. "I could get help and rescue you."

"What if you couldn't get away and the monks found you? They would put you right back in here."

"But they don't know I'm here," she said. "I could just show up and say my car broke down or something."

"You're limping and all banged up. They would have questions. You don't have any identification. It could be risky."

Juliet's heart sank. Then after several seconds, she had an idea. "There might be another way to go."

"What?"

"Not what: who."

"I don't understand."

"You could ask Trevor to come with us. He's a guy. He would know how to drive the truck."

Damian stared at her. "I told you, he doesn't want to leave."

"If he's your friend, he'll help you."

"No. He'd try to stop me."

His statement stunned her. "Why in the name of God would he do that? I'd assume that he would want you to escape."

"No. He wants me to stay so he won't be alone."

"That's pretty selfish. Now I hate him even more. Why does he want to stay?"

"He likes it here."

Likes it?

"Then he's out of his mind!" said Juliet. "After being stuck here for twelve years, wouldn't he welcome the chance to escape?"

"He committed some crimes before he got here. He's afraid that he'll have to go to jail."

This gets weirder and weirder.

"What kind of crimes?"

"Selling drugs. Robbing houses. He told me he was a bad kid. His brother had to go to jail for a year. He lived with his brother. One time he broke into an apartment and the owner was there. He got into a fight. He hurt the guy. He only took the job here to hide because it's so remote. He's changed. He's a good guy."

"My guess is that if he didn't hurt anybody, the police would give him some slack. I mean, being here for twelve years is like being locked up. And if he's a good guy he should be happy that you've found a way out. Ask him to come with us. Let him come down the mountain with us. Let him show me how to drive, and if he doesn't want to escape, he can come back here."

"Because of his damaged foot and leg, he couldn't climb down the mountain himself. I'd have to carry him. This isn't a good idea."

"He's your only chance. He's *my* only chance of getting out of here. You need to ask him, Damian."

"I... "

"Besides, if we can escape and reach the media and you can be heard, you'll tell them about this place and it'll be swarming with cops. All the giants and the abnormals and Trevor will be free too. One way or another, he'll be able to get out."

"I never thought of that."

"Ask him, Damian. Please go now and tell him the plan."

"I don't know."

"Okay. Here's another idea. Take me down. If I can drive the truck we'll go. If I can't you can go back up. I'll call my brother and The Habitat Project and we'll come back to rescue you. We'll rescue everybody. What do you say to that?"

Damian considered the idea.

"When you say everybody, who do you mean?"

"The normal-sized people and all the giants."

"What if the giants don't want to be rescued?" said Damian.

The question stunned Juliet. "Why would you say that?"

"My uncle Pete wouldn't want it. I don't think most of the giants would want to be free."

"They don't have to. Look, Damian, we have to get this resolved. You need to talk to Trevor. Maybe you're wrong. Maybe he's changed his mind. He never had the opportunity to escape until now. You have to ask him. If he says no, he says no and we'll be on our own. I'll try to drive the freakin' truck."

"Alright. I'll ask him tomorrow."

"Thank you," she said. "Okay, let's assume he says yes. What are we gonna do when we get out? What about gas?"

"What about it?"

"Will the truck be filled up?"

"I don't know."

"What about money?"

"I don't have any."

"Neither do I. You buried my purse with the plane. I had over two hundred dollars and a credit card. We'll need cash. Not only for gasoline, but for food and a map, although we'll probably just have to drive south. And if the monks, or I should say, *when* the monks figure out that you're gone, we'll be an easy target, which means we'll have to get another truck. Probably right away."

Damian looked confused. "How will we do that?"

"How else? Steal one, I guess."

"Do you know how to do that?"

"No. But we'll have to figure it out. We'll probably have to take the back roads."

"What are back roads?" Damian asked.

"I'm not sure. I've seen lots of movies where people are running away from something and they take the back roads. I guess they're roads off the beaten path." She changed the subject. "How long do you think you'll be able to stay curled up in the truck? You'll have to get out and stretch once in a while. That would draw attention. No gas, no money, no real destination. Your plan isn't very well thought out, Damien."

"I guess it isn't," he said gloomily.

"It's more like a rough outline of a plan, but at least you tried."

"Thank you."

"Let's say Trevor wants to come with us and that he can drive the truck. We'll go until we find a phone, probably at a rest stop. I think those are every twenty-five or thirty miles or something. I'll call my brother and tell him I'm alive and about you."

Damian looked concerned. "What will you tell him about me?"

"That you're a giant, that you're articulate and intelligent and nice and kind and that you and your family and a whole race of giants have been held prisoner for like a hundred years. He'll probably think I'm out of my mind, but once he processes it, he'll believe me. He won't know how to get media attention, but I'm sure a call to CNN in New York will get the ball rolling."

"I'm still not sure I want to do that. I just want to be with my people at Mont Blanc."

"Assuming they're there."

Damian held out his right hand and pointed at the ring. "This ring means that giants will be there!" he shouted, then softly he said, "It's the only place I have to go."

Juliet felt sorry for him.

"You can't get there unless you get out of here, Damian! That's the first objective of your new plan. Okay?"

"Okay."

"The way I see it, you can come with me. I'll be your spokesperson. I was a reporter for my school paper and I starred in a nine-minute documentary. I have a presence. Everybody said I should go into journalism. I know how to write a news story. I know how to talk on camera. I'll tell the world about you."

"The world scares me."

"This place scares *me*."

"If I did, what would happen to me?"

"I... I don't know for sure, but I promise you that I won't let them hurt you."

She reached out her right hand and touched his face.

"How could you stop them, Juliet?"

"It wouldn't be just me. My brother isn't famous or anything, but he's a good kid. He has a lot of integrity. He's a salt-of-the-earth kind of kid. With him and me backing you up, you'll have a chance."

"I don't know."

"Damian, it's our only chance. It's *your* only chance to escape."

He pondered the idea for several seconds, then said, "It's like what you said. Better to die trying."

"Yes! Okay, let's do this as soon as possible. Let's leave tomorrow."

"Tomorrow?"

"Yes."

"Are you strong enough, luv?"

"I could go right now."

"I have to say goodbye to my uncle."

"He'll be all alone when you go. How will he feel about that?"

"He's old. He knows I want to get out. He'll understand."

"Why wouldn't he want to escape?" asked Juliet.

"He's always accepted his fate. Live here or out there, being imprisoned as a freak, studied by scientists. He didn't buy into finding our people in France. He was afraid. No way he'd go."

"But you're not afraid. You know in your heart that you want to run. Let's do it together."

"Okay."

"With or without Trevor."

"Okay."

"We'll leave tomorrow. Are you good with that?"

"Yes."

"What time will we be going?"

"Dusk."

"Why so late?"

"We can't go in the daytime because the workers will be there. At dusk, the place is shut down."

Juliet nodded in agreement. "Okay then."

"Meanwhile, you need to rest up."

~~~~~~

Damian went outside to think. His thoughts turned to escape. Now that it was being discussed, he was in a panic. He always knew he couldn't do it alone.

Damian never thought the opportunity would come, which added to his frustration. How could he find someone who could drive? He knew that Trevor could drive, but that he wouldn't leave. It depressed him and ate away at his soul.

He'd been waiting for this chance for two years, ever since his escape route came to him like a gift from God.

He had gotten into the habit of going into the territory belonging to Martin and his giants, climbing the mountain as high as he could go and staring out at the countryside. Because the sheer flatness of the wall made climbing down impossible, he would get depressed and frustrated.

But that all changed the day the fissure in the mountainside happened. He was sitting in his usual place, just looking out when suddenly, there was a rumble and within seconds the rocks cracked open and magically there was a way out. More accurately, there was a way down the mountain and into the farmland where the berries grew.

The fissure made an easy path down the mountain and it was so small no one on the ground could see it. He climbed down it the first time that night and from that moment on he began thinking of escape.

He wasn't sure what to do about Trevor. Despite the fact that they hadn't gotten along for the last two years, they were like brothers. He knew that if he and

Juliet made it out and if Juliet was right, he would most likely never see Trevor again. They would tell the media everything and police or somebody would come to the reserve and find the abnormals and the giants.

He was afraid to tell Trevor about his plans because he knew he wouldn't like it. He would be angry. He might try to stop him.

But he knew he had to tell him and ask for his help.

He decided to pay Trevor a visit.

~~~~~~

When Damian got to Trevor's cave, he found him reading by torchlight. Trevor was shocked to see him. Damian almost never visited at night, even when things were good between them.

"Is everything alright with Juliet?" Trevor asked, concern in his voice.

"Yeah. I just wanted to thank you for everything you said to her. She needed to hear it."

"I hope she won't hate me forever. Did you talk to her on my behalf? Did you tell her I'm a good guy?"

"Not yet. I will. The time has to be right. She's still dealing with the fact that she's here."

"I guess so."

"I'll get to it."

Trevor nodded. He sensed that something was bothering Damian.

178

"What's going on?"

"I have to tell you something."

"Yeah."

"I found a way out of here." Trevor froze.

"Juliet and I are leaving tomorrow."

"What? How does she fit into this?"

"We need your help," Damian said firmly.

"Wait a minute. She's been here four days and you're going to escape with her?"

"I found the escape route two years ago."

Trevor was dumbfounded. "Why didn't you tell me?"

"What for? All you would've done is try to talk me out of escaping."

"For your own good. Where is it?"

"A fissure in the mountain overlooking the plant, Damian. I can barely see them, but they can't see me because the opening is tucked in the stone."

"Why would you not have told me?"

"Because I needed somebody to drive one of the monk's trucks and I knew you wouldn't have done it, so why bother?"

"Drive one of the monk's trucks? You've thought this through."

"A little."

"So, Juliet is gonna drive the truck?"

"That's the problem. She doesn't know how to drive stick shift. It was her idea to ask you."

"Really? Does she know about my past?"

"A little."

"What's your plan, to hide in the truck and be driven to freedom?"

"Yes."

"You'll be driven to your death." Trevor shrugged and shook his head back and forth. "How do you know you can fit in the truck?"

"I climbed down the mountain and measured them. I can fit."

"You climbed *down*?" He was incredulous.

"Yes."

"Let me guess why you came back? Because you didn't have anywhere to go?"

"Yes."

"So, where you gonna go this time?"

"Juliet is taking care of that. She's gonna get media attention. And her brother will help too."

Trevor shook his head back and forth. "Her brother? How old is he, twelve?"

"She was going to be a runner. She said she would rather die than stay here. So, I told her how I found a fissure on the north side of the mountain. I've climbed down a bunch of times."

"Jesus. I just can't believe you didn't tell me that. Was it hard to come back?"

"No. Because without transportation there was nowhere to go. Will you help us, Trevor? If you don't want to make a run for it, all you have to do is start the truck and show Juliet how to work the stick shift. Then, I'll take you back up the mountain."

"Even if I helped you, there are no guarantees you'd get away. I know where you want to go. She won't be able to take you to France. One way or another, you'll wind up in some kind of research hospital or prison."

"She doesn't think so."

"She's seventeen! And so are you. Seventeen-year-olds don't think clearly."

"She made me realize something, Trevor. That it's better to die trying to escape than to do nothing at all."

The comment hung in the air.

"She's a child, Damian! And you're listening to her?"

"Will you help me, Trevor? If it's yes, I'll tell you our plan. If it's no, then this will be goodbye."

Damian stared Trevor in the eyes.

"She's wrong, Damian. Being alive is always better."

"Once she and I get in the truck and go, we'll be out. She thinks we'll make it to New York."

"If she can drive the truck."

"Yes."

"What if she can't?"

Damian said nothing.

"I'm not going to help you die, Damian. And that's what will happen to you and probably to her too. You'll both be dead."

"Juliet doesn't think that will happen."

"Oh, she knows so much. Let me talk to her."

"No."

"Let's go right now. I'll try to reason with her."

"She hates you, Trevor."

The statement caught Trevor off guard. He didn't know what to say. "Because I was truthful."

"You could've gone easier on her. It was a lot to take in."

"Okay."

"Then, this is goodbye."

"Damian, if you make it out and if they don't kill you or imprison you, is your plan to bring the cops or whoever back here?"

"Yes. I guess."

"Don't tell them about me."

"Why not?"

"Because I don't have anything to go back to except prison."

"You don't know that."

"Yes, I do."

"Isn't being here for twelve years punishment enough?"

"I can't take that chance, Damian."

"What about your brother?"

"I don't know that he's even living in our house anymore."

"He might be."

"And he might not. Goodbye, Damian."

"Goodbye, Trevor."

Damian took a last look at his only friend, turned and walked away.

The next person he needed to say goodbye to was his uncle Pete. He wondered how he would take the news. He decided to wait until morning.

~~~~~~

When Trevor woke up the next day, he was sick to his stomach. He had watched Damian leave. Maybe the only true friend he ever had. Not only would he be losing him, but with Juliet going with Damian, he would lose his last chance at love, creating a life with someone and building a family. Should he let them go, probably condemning Damian to his death, or tell Abbot Gassner the truth, condemning Juliet to nothing less than lifelong imprisonment for which she would hate him even more.

He had a big decision to make, and he didn't have much time to make it and take action.

DAY

4

CHAPTER

20

Juliet lay awake most of the night thinking about her encounter with the old women who'd been imprisoned in the reserve so long. She felt sorry for them, but she knew that she couldn't have a life like theirs. The thought of spending every day of her life in the reserve continued to petrify her. She wanted to leave right now. That she had to wait all day, until dusk, gave her a headache.

Her thoughts turned to Damian. She couldn't believe how nice he was. She found herself wishing that he were normal-sized. They would make a great couple. She never thought like that. She'd had a few boyfriends during her high school years, but they were all casual. She wasn't interested in a relationship. She wanted to go to college and learn everything she could. Then she wanted to move on to graduate school, travel through Europe and eventually build an illustrious career. In what field she wasn't quite sure of, but she knew it would be wonderful. Maybe she would get married one day, but not before she turned 30. Or even 35.

But Damian affected her. After only four days, she couldn't get him out of her head. She tried to imagine him at six feet tall. Normal-sized. She wished that they could walk in the forest like regular couples, holding hands, talking about the different lives and experiences they'd had. Or their dreams. She had so many. And Damian only had one.

This is crazy. Why am I thinking these thoughts? He's a giant. He's three times as big as me. How can I fall in love with a giant?

Based on what Damian had told her, she was certain that he was most likely wrong about giants living at Mont Blanc, but she chose not to tell him.

If he could get her out of this place, she would worry about helping him later. She knew that once they were in the truck it would only be a matter of time before she found a phone. She would call Greg first to let him know she was all right. She considered having him call the media, but decided that he didn't have the aggressive personality needed to get through the news desks at the various television networks.

She did.

She decided that after alerting her brother that she was safe, she would be the one to call. She would know how to talk to people and get the reaction she wanted.

Then she and Damian, together, would expose what the Catholic Church had done to the giants.

~~~~~~

The first thing Damian did was go to his uncle to tell him he was leaving. He knew that Pete would want him to get to the point quickly.

"Uncle Pete, I found a way out."

"Of what?"

"The reserve. I found it two years ago."

Pete just stared at him sorrowfully. "Where?"

"A fissure on the north side of the mountain. It gives clear passage down, easy passage. I couldn't do anything about it because I needed help. Juliet is going to help me escape."

Pete stared at Damian. "Juliet?" He shook his head back and forth. "They'll kill you both."

"She has a plan."

"Plans rarely work."

"She thinks it can."

"Something always goes wrong, Damian."

"She made me realize that it'll be better to try than to spend the rest of my life here."

"What if you succeed?"

"I don't understand."

"What if you escape and they don't kill you? You'll tell them about this place, right?"

"Yes. I'll come back and save you."

"I don't want to be saved," said Pete. "I want to live out my life here."

"But if I can free you --"

"For what? What would I do? Where would I live? At least here I can be myself. You should think about that, Damian. Even if you get free and you tell the world about us, you will still have to live among the abnormals. You will never fit in."

Damian considered the remark. "I'll live at Mont Blanc."

"If you can find a way there and if your mother's story is true, I wish you well."

"Why wouldn't you think it was true?"

"Your mother wanted to believe it. She needed to believe. My life is here. I lived here and I will die here. When will you be going?"

"Tonight."

Pete sighed. "I can see that your mind is made up. I wish you good luck, Damian." Pete leaned forward and gave his nephew a hug. "Remember this: I don't want to be rescued. I don't think any of the giants will want to be rescued. Except for Martin. He might."

"Why Martin?"

"But he won't want to go to Mont Blanc. He'll want to attack the Catholic Church. Or worse."

Damian looked at his uncle. "What do you mean?"

"He'll want revenge."

"How?"

"By killing as many monks as he can."

The statement shocked Damian.

Then Pete said, "Can't say that I blame him."

CHAPTER

21

At seven-thirty that night, Damian decided it would be safe to go. He carried Juliet on his right shoulder and moved purposely up the mountain. She was surprisingly quiet as she anticipated being out of the reserve and having her life back. She felt safe and comforted holding on to him.

After twenty-six minutes, they came to where the fissure in the mountain was. Damian put her on the ground.

"We're here."

Even before Damian set her down, Juliet could see the gaping hole in the rocks.

"And this just, like, happened?" she asked.

"Yes. Nature. Erosion."

She moved closer to the hole and looked down. "I can see everything. It's all tiny, but I can make out things. Just think, tomorrow we'll be down there."

"I hope you won't abandon me."

"Why would you say that, Damian? I'm here to help you."

"Once you're out of this place, you won't want to come back," said Damian.

"I wouldn't go without you."

"You say that now, but once you taste freedom again, you won't willingly come back."

"You've been so kind to me. What kind of person would I be if I didn't want to come back?"

"You'll run screaming away and I'll be stuck down there."

He's right. Why would I come back to this horrible place? I'm a terrible person. I owe him my life. I won't leave him. I can't leave him.

"I won't leave you, Damian."

She reached out her right hand and touched him.

"I'll understand if you do," he said.

"I said I was going to help you and I will."

"Thank you, Juliet."

"Come here, Damian. Crouch down in front of me."

He did so.

"Come closer. Bring you face as close as you possible can."

He did so.

"Now pick me up and bring me to you lips."

He did so.

"I'm going to kiss you."

"I don't know how to kiss a girl. The only person I ever kissed was my mother."

"Just pucker your lips and bring me to them."

He did so.

Damian held Juliet as close to his lips as he could.

"I'm going to lean in and give you a kiss."

She did so.

She could only kiss a small part of his lower lip, but it was enough to make her point.

"If you were smaller and I were bigger we could kiss all the time," she said, then kissed him again. "But this will have to be enough. You need to find a girl your own size."

"Where? Out there?"

Juliet said nothing.

Damian moved closer to the fissure. "You can see the trucks in the distance."

"They're so far away. They look like tiny dots. How can you see them?"

"Giants have superior vision. Superior hearing too. We can communicate through signals we make with our mouths. When we get down there, no one will be watching you. Everyone moves slowly. The drivers go into a small building and pick up the keys to the trucks. When they come back, they return them."

"How do you know this?" said Juliet.

"I watched them enough times to make a guess."

Suddenly, Juliet was concerned. "So, you could be wrong."

"There's probably someone inside who assigns them or gives out the keys. When you go inside, try to get the keys to truck number twelve. I've watched the building enough times to see that they have a system. A driver goes in and comes out in like thirty or forty seconds. I think he must ask for the key to a truck, and then, he goes."

"Still more guessing. What if I have to sign in or show some identification?"

"I don't know what to say."

"And why number twelve?"

"The number twelve truck is parked far enough away from the warehouse that no one will see me get inside."

"I thought you said no one's around."

"There hasn't been, except one day."

"What if truck number twelve isn't available?"

"It always is. Every day I checked it was there."

She was getting irritated. "But what if it isn't? You have to plan for the unexpected, Damian."

He pondered the question for several seconds. "Then take whichever one they give you. But try for number twelve."

"Okay." She was about to ask Damian how difficult it was going to be do go down the mountain when a deep male voice that he'd heard many times before bellowed.

"What you do here?"

They both turned around and saw Victor standing twenty feet away.

"We're taking a walk," said Damian.

"A walk up mountain in dark?" He moved closer to the fissure. "I never see this hole before." He stepped closer. "I see down. Climbing down easy from here."

"It's too steep. You'd fall and break your bloody neck."

"It not steep at all, said Victor. "I could go down mountain easy in daytime. This place new. I tell Martin. It a way out."

"To what?"

"Huh?"

"Where would you go?"

"To be free."

"But where would you go?" said Damian, not quite believing that he was making the same arguments Pete and Trevor gave him. "You've spent every day of your life in the woods. Out there is civilization and there is no room for giants." He paused to let the statement sink in. "You'll be killed or taken prisoner and locked away as a freak."

Victor scrunched up his face. "I get Martin."

"I'd say the same thing to Martin. If any of us try to escape, our lives will be over. Do you want your life to end, Victor?"

"No."

"How would you feed yourself? Where would you live? Your life is in here. So is mine."

Victor considered the idea. "But girl's not. Her life out there."

"That's why I'm going to let her go. I'm going to take her down and set her free."

"No!" Victor bellowed. "I need a cook."

Juliet shook her head.

Not this bullshit again.

"She's young. She has a right to her life and we have to live ours, hidden away."

"I tell Martin. He not like this. He knows we need her." He backed away.

"Go ahead. Tell him."

"This not right, Damian. I go get Martin now."

Victor turned around and looked down. Standing in front of him was Trevor blocking his way. He held his bow and arrow aimed up at Victor. He was breathing heavily and sweating.

"What you want, Trevor?" said Victor.

Trevor fired an arrow into Victor's right big toe. He screamed with pain.

"Get him," shouted Trevor.

Suddenly, Damian punched Victor in the side of the head, stunning him, then he hit him three more times, knocking him out. He fell to the ground unconscious.

"How did you make it up the mountain?" asked Damian, glancing at Trevor's foot.

"Very slowly," said Trevor.

"Then you changed your mind?" asked Juliet.

"No. I'll help you on one condition. I'll show Juliet how to handle stick shift and you two can be on your own. If you manage to wind up free, you have to promise not to mention me."

The remark stunned both Damian and Juliet.

"Why not?" asked Juliet.

"I've been in hiding for the last twelve years, and I want to stay that way. I want you to drop me off somewhere, and then forget about me."

"Where?" asked Damian.

"When you brought up my brother, it got me thinking. He might still be living in our house, the place we grew up in. After my mother died, we both inherited it. If he's there, I can stay with him for the time being. I'm going to assume a new identity. Alright?"

"What if he's not alive?" asked Juliet. "What if he moved?"

"I don't know. I'll find a way to get by."

"How?" asked Damian. "You'll be just like me. Entering a world you don't really know anymore. Come with us. Help me take a stand against the Catholic Church."

"I've made up my mind."

Damian had learned that his friend was stubborn. Once he makes up his mind about something that was it. "Whatever you want, Trevor."

"We'll have to go down soon." He gestured towards Victor. "When he comes to, he'll go get Martin and tell him there's a way out. Martin will want to follow."

"Why?" asked Juliet. "Where would he go? What would he do?"

"He wouldn't go far. I think he'd go find the Abbot, kill him and maybe every other monk he could get his hands on. We have to go. Are you ready, Juliet?"

"Yes."

"Damian?"

He nodded yes.

"Let's go," said Trevor.

Damian lifted Juliet and swung her around to his shoulder and did the same with Trevor on his right. They both clung to Damian's collar as he climbed carefully down the mountain.

Juliet looked over at Trevor. "Thank you for doing this."

"I'm doing it for Damian." He looked away. He was done being nice to her. His thoughts were on reconnecting with his brother and starting a new life.

~~~~~~

When they reached level ground, Damian put his fellow escapees down and they headed toward the trucks, which were about a hundred yards away.

"The trucks are all unlocked, both the driver's and passenger side," said Damian. "Each truck is assigned a specific parking space, by number, so we have to make sure that the keys you get belong to the truck I'll be inside of. Let's go to number twelve now."

"Why?" said Trevor.

"We can wait inside it until morning."

"Why don't I just break into the building and steal the keys?" said Trevor.

Juliet said, "What if they have an alarm? That's all we'd need."

"Are you sure they don't lock the trucks?" said Trevor.

"Yes. I watched the drivers go to their trucks and open the doors."

They crept slowly to the truck. Even though it was still dark Trevor was taken aback by the design on the truck. Each side had drawings of jellies and jams and a smiling monk logo flanking a prominent rendering that was sure to gather attention: a gigantic fat smiling monk.

"This is bad," Trevor said.

Juliet noticed it too.

"Are you kidding me? As soon as it's daylight, we'll be at risk."

"Can't we drive on the back roads?" asked Juliet.

"If we were taking a Sunday drive with no one chasing us and we weren't in a truck.

Trevor opened the back door and looked at Damian. "Get in, buddy."

Damian climbed into the back of the truck, stretching out with his head facing where the drivers sat. There was a wall dividing them.

"We probably won't be able to talk to you while we're driving because of the divide. You gonna be okay?"

"Yeah."

"We'll get in here with you. We should all try to sleep. Juliet, after you?"

He helped her into the truck, then he climbed in, then they stared at each other in silence.

Damian tried to make himself comfortable, lying on the steel floor. He felt oddly at ease. He couldn't get used to having his body touch steel. He had never experienced the sensation because he had never seen anything made of steel.

He took a deep breath.

So, this is freedom

As he twirled the gold ring on his finger round and round, he wondered if he would ever get to Mont Blanc.

~~~~~~

Victor woke up five hours later with a pain in his toe from Trevor's arrow, a throbbing headache and a bloody nose. He struggled to get up. He stood, felt wobbly, walked to the fissure and looked down.

Damian free. He not come back. He free.

He turned and made his way to Martin's cave.

As he moved, what Damian had said to him about being free stayed in his head.

He rarely thought about ever getting out of the reserve, but now that he had the opportunity, he wasn't sure if he wanted it.

He would ask Martin what he should do.

Martin always knew best. He would do whatever Martin told him to.

~~~~~~

Trevor woke up first. There was virtually no air in the cargo area. He heard Damian snoring loudly and Juliet breathing softly. He wondered what time it was so he opened the door. It was the break of dawn.

He woke Juliet.

"It's time to go," he said softly.

As she rubbed the sleep from her eyes, she nodded her head and said, "Okay."

Trevor nudged Damian. "Hey! Wake up."

The young giant tried to stretch, but had no room to do so.

"How you feeling?"

The giant tried to maneuver in the claustrophobic space. "My back is sore."

"It's gonna get even more sore. Juliet and I will get in the front."

"Okay."

Trevor turned to Juliet. "Let's go."

They slipped out of the back of the truck. While Juliet went to the front and got inside, Trevor prepared to shut the door, which would lock Damian in.

"Closing the door now."

"Okay."

"Once we get to a phone, it'll all be over," said Trevor.

"Will it?" said Damian.

"You're out of the reserve. It'll be nothing but up from here."

Damian didn't respond.

Trevor closed and locked Damian in, then went around to the front and got inside.

"Now we wait," said Trevor.

"Trevor?" said Juliet. "I know you were trying to help me when you told me about the rules and how the reserve was inescapable, but I couldn't process it. I'm sorry if I was mean to you."

"I get it. That's behind us now. One of the things you learn being a prisoner is that you never look back, only forward.

CHAPTER

22

Twenty-eight minutes later at six a.m., a lone man made his way to the garage, unlocked the door and entered. He carried a thermos.

"That must be the guy with the keys," said Juliet.

"Yeah," said Trevor. "I'll go in now, before he gets settled, maybe throw him off guard." Trevor opened the door. As he slid out he said, "Wish me luck."

Juliet smiled at him.

When Trevor got inside, he didn't know what to expect. He saw an old man pouring himself a cup of coffee from the thermos.

"Key for truck number twelve," Trevor said softly.

The old man didn't look up. It was as if he hadn't heard him.

He tried again, this time a little louder.

"Number twelve, please."

"I heard you," the guy said, still not looking up, then went to a board behind his counter and picked up a set of keys. "You're not the regular guy."

"He called in sick. I'm new. I got a call last night to take the number twelve truck."

"You're early."

"Couldn't sleep."

He tossed the keys to Trevor and said, "Go easy. The camshaft has been acting up. Only has a quarter of a tank so you better fill it up."

"Okay." Trevor nodded, walked out and headed back to truck number twelve.

He got inside. "We have a problem. The truck only has a quarter-of-a-tank of gas." He looked ahead about forty yards away and saw four gas pumps, but he had no idea how the system worked.

"Let's use one of those gas things," said Juliet.

"I don't know if the drivers have a code they need to use. I think we should just get the hell out of here and worry about gas later."

"Maybe they don't use a code."

"A quarter-of-a-tank will probably take us seventy-five miles or so."

"I don't even know which side of the truck the gas tank is on."

"So"

"If I'm pretending to be a driver of one of these things I should know where it is," he said with exasperation. "And if the pumps need a code, I can't just walk up to one and stand there like an idiot."

Juliet considered what he said. "Can't you at least *try*?"

Trevor shrugged, shook his head and snapped, "Okay."

He turned on the ignition. It didn't turn over. He tried it again. Nothing. One more time, then it happened. He put the gearshift in Drive and guided the truck shakily to the gas tanks. As he reached for the door handle, Juliet said, "Good luck."

"I'll need *great* luck for this," he snarled.

Trevor slid out of the truck and approached the pumps. He knew immediately that he would need a credit card of some sort because the pumps were unlike any he'd ever seen. Unlike those he was used to, which provided slots to insert cash, this one had a place to insert something. Under it were the words emblazoned on the pump:

DRIVERS

MAKE SURE CARD IS INSERTED CORRECTLY

Below that was a diagram showing the proper way to slide the card in.

Trevor turned away and went back to the truck.

"I was right. You need a card to get in." He looked irritated.

"At least we tried," said Gretchen.

"Let's move," said Trevor. He looked through the window on the separation between the cargo space and the driver's and saw Damian curled up.

"How you doing back there?"

"Tight," said Damian. "But I'm okay."

"So, are you gonna show me how to drive the stick shift, Trevor?" she said.

"No need to. This truck is automatic. You didn't need me after all."

"But this has more dials and knobs than I've ever seen."

"All you need to do is put it in drive and go. I'll take some time to walk you through it when we stop."

"Okay."

"We'll need to get money for gas," said Trevor.

She looked concerned. "How will we do that?"

Trevor sighed. "We'll have to rob somebody." He sighed again. "I'm free for two minutes and I already revert to my old habits."

"Will people get hurt?" asked Juliet.

"That depends. Nobody likes to give up their money."

I hope no one gets hurt.

"Are you ready?" said Trevor.

"Yes."

He turned on the ignition.

"You ready, Damian?"

"Yes."

"Here goes."

Juliet turned around and looked at Damian through the tiny window.

"You're beginning the adventure of your life." She leaned toward him. He maneuvered his right hand and touched the tip of her finger through the window. They smiled at each other.

Getting out of St. Alban's was easy because of the time. The workers were all going about their business. Everything was normal. Trevor maneuvered the truck slowly out of the grounds and onto a road that would take them to the Interstate. He remembered driving on it twelve years ago. It looked exactly the same.

"Which way is New York City?" asked Juliet.

"I remember the freeway being about five miles to the left," said Trevor. "Let's get the hell out of here."

He turned left and headed out.

"Feels good to drive," said Trevor. "I wonder what the monks did with my car. Used Honda. Good vehicle."

Juliet looked at Damian.

"You're free!"

He smiled at her tentatively.

"Why does that scare me?"

"Very soon you'll get to tell your story, Damian," she said. "And I'll be at your side to help. So will my dad." She turned to Trevor. "And maybe Trevor will too."

"No. I'll be leaving you as soon as we can switch trucks, then I'll remain anonymous. We need to find a cell phone or a phone booth. Of course, it would help if we had money or a credit card to pay for a call. And you can make a collect call."

"I've never done that," said Juliet.

"Really?"

"What's a collect call?" asked Damian.

"It's when you call someone and ask them to pay for it," said Trevor. "There will be phone booths at rest stops."

"Maybe not," said Juliet. "Phone booths are pretty much obsolete."

"Are you kidding me?"

"Everybody has a smart phone."

Trevor shook his head back and forth. "I've been away a long time."

"Our best bet will be to find someone who can lend me their phone, then I'll call my brother."

"What does a phone look like?" asked Damian.

"I could ask the same question," said Trevor. "The last cell phone I owned was a flip phone."

"Those are long gone," said Juliet. "Like I said, everybody uses a smart phone."

"Why do they call it that?"

"Because it pretty much contains everything in your life."

Suddenly, the truck started jumping.

"Let's not talk right now," said Trevor. "I need to get comfortable driving this thing."

"Fine."

As they cruised along the road, Juliet focused on what to do once she got a phone.

First, I'll call Greg.

Then I'll call CNN in New York.

Then I'll call the police.

Then I'll call The Habitat Project and let them know I'm alright.

Then I'll call my dad.

Then I'll work on what I'm going to tell the world!

CHAPTER

23

When the driver of truck number twelve requested its keys and they weren't available, a call was made to Brother Thomas who suspected something, though he wasn't exactly sure what, was up.

The monk made the trek from the main monastery to the garage on the other side of Hammerhead Mountain. The old man who gave out the keys to the truck was questioned and said that a worker had come in, said he was replacing the usual driver, asked for the keys to truck number twelve and left. There was nothing unusual about it. That he hadn't recognized him meant nothing because new people were always being hired.

It didn't occur to Brother Thomas that a giant had escaped. He assumed a new employee had stolen the truck. But why? An empty truck? They'd had trouble with workers occasionally; every two or three years an alcoholic or drug addict made his way into a job.

"He's had maybe a half-hour start," said the old man.

"I'll call the police and have them put out an All Points Bulletin," said Brother George, then he turned and went outside to where truck number twelve had been parked. He studied the empty space for several seconds, shrugged his narrow shoulders, then was about to leave, when he saw it in the dirt.

A footprint.

Huge.

He was so taken aback to see it that, at first, he didn't know what to make of it, but then he knew it belonged to a giant. He realized that a giant had escaped.

There was another and another and another, and they were next to a set of two normal-sized persons footprints.

Brother Thomas called Abbot Gassner immediately. "Abbot, I think... I think a giant has escaped."

"What are you talking about? That's impossible."

"I'm looking at the footprints," he said. "A bunch of them."

Gassner sat up straight.

"He stole one of our trucks and... "

"Wait. How could a giant drive a truck?"

"You didn't let me finish. Besides his footprints there are two other sets of smaller ones. Undoubtedly from the normal-sized prisoners."

"They aren't prisoners," snapped Gassner.

"My guess is that one of them is driving the truck, Abbot Gassner."

"Obviously one of them is driving the truck."

"Should I call the police?"

"No! Call no one. Are you at the garage?"

"Yes."

"I'll be right there."

Abbot Gassner was in such a state of shock and anxiety, he didn't know what to do first, despite the fact that he'd been given specific instructions. He was given a name of a man in Vatican City, which he had on his iPhone under V for Vatican. He had never been given any real training as to what to do in the event something like this happened. He had been assured that the reserve was escape-proof.

He had a bicycle that he kept for exercise, which he rode to the garage. Brother Thomas was waiting, standing over the giant footprint.

Abbot Gassner got off his bike and without looking at the younger brother or speaking to him, checked out the footprints.

"I never saw a giant up close," Gassner said. "These footprints are enormous."

"The other prints look so tiny compared to his."

Gassner checked them out as well. "We have to stop them."

"Should I call the police *now*?" asked Brother Thomas.

"No! We are not calling the police. Do you want a state trooper to find a giant in the truck?"

"I... No, Abbot, of course not. I don't know what I was thinking."

"We can't expose what we've been doing here?"

"No, Abbot. I just thought that we needed to do something."

"We will. What do you do when you need to talk to Trevor?"

"Ring the horn three times."

With his heart pounding, Abbot Gassner got back on his bike and headed directly to the private entrance gate to the reserve on the far side of Hammerhead Mountain. He rang the horn three times, then out of nervousness, he rang it three more times.

He knew it would take Trevor some time to get there.

He took a deep breath and prepared to call his contact at The Vatican, a man he'd never spoken to.

Gassner knew that his demeanor had a tendency to put people off, but it was the way he survived in the Order. He thought those who feared him would find it amusing that he was like them when it came to his Vatican contact.

He was given instructions never to call unless it was a true emergency and he'd obeyed that. He knew that today was indeed an emergency of the highest order.

He'd been given a special phone belonging to Archbishop Andre Vircuzi.

Gassner rarely thought about the giants. After a few years, it was as if they weren't even there. The only one he knew anything about was number 647 because he was the youngest and last giant to be born. When number 647 died it would be the end of the giants. But this? His escaping. He had never imagined it possible.

He pressed Archbishop Vircuzi's number.

After the first ring, a man picked up the line and in Italian, said, "You have reached the office of Archbishop Vircuzi. How may I help you?"

"I am Abbot James Gassner of St. Alban's Monastery in the States. I was told to call the Archbishop only in an emergency. I have a major emergency. I need to speak to him immediately."

"Please hold for the Archbishop."

There were several seconds of silence until a voice came on.

"Abbot Gassner, what is your emergency?" a deep voice asked.

"One of our giants has escaped."

Vircuzi sat up. "How?"

"I'm not sure how he got out. There's something else."

"What?"

"The giant wasn't alone."

Vircuzi stood up and began pacing around his office. "You mean that more than one giant escaped?"

"No. Two of our normal-sized people. I don't know who they are, but I'm trying to find out. I saw their footprints. One from the giant, and two normal-sized. They escaped in one of our trucks. Archbishop, that is essentially what I know so far."

"How long ago did this happen, Abbot?"

"Half-an-hour to forty-five minutes."

"Their plan is obviously to go public."

"That was my inclination too."

"The question is how will they do it? And where? And whether or not they have allies on the outside who can help them."

"I doubt that, Archbishop."

"Why?"

"The two that are accompanying the giant have been secluded in the reserve for many years. They had no way to reach anyone on the outside."

"But now that they're out, they'll try to look for family members and friends they can call who will be only too anxious to help them. Is there any way to find out who went with the giant?"

"I'm waiting to talk to the person who acts as a go-between for me."

"What is his name?"

"Trevor."

Vircuzi wrote down the name.

"How long has he been there?"

"I believe twelve years. He should be here shortly."

"How long have you been there, Abbot Gassner?"

"Twenty-eight years."

"How could they have stolen a truck?"

"I haven't figured that out yet."

"This is quite troubling. I'll call the Templar in your area."

"Albert Sulpience?"

"Yes. I'll go over what the next step should be and have him phone you. Do you know Mister Sulpience?"

"Yes. We had a few incidents over the years."

"Incidents?"

"Escape attempts. He solved the problem."

"By giants?"

"No. By new captives."

"He is a very capable man."

"Archbishop?"

"Yes?"

"If Sulpience finds the giant, what will he do to him?"

Vircuzi did not hesitate with his answer. "He'll have to eliminate all three."

"What about the remaining giants in the reserve and the people who've been held there?" asked Gassner. "What do we do with them? Especially if six-forty-seven manages to go public."

"The same."

"I beg your pardon?"

"I want them all eliminated, Abbot. Sulpience and his men will handle it. Find out how six-forty-seven escaped and block the exit. We don't want anyone else getting out. Any other questions, Abbot Gassner?"

"No, Archbishop. Thank you."

"Wait for a call from Sulpience before you do anything else."

"Yes, Archbishop."

They hung up. Abbot Gassner rang the horn that called Trevor three more times, then his brain began filtering through the primary ramification a giant on the loose could mean:

He or the people he was with could tell the world what the Catholic Church had done. And what he himself had been a willing part of.

Dearest God, have mercy on my soul.

CHAPTER

24

Even though it was an automatic transmission and Trevor was reasonably comfortable driving the truck, the vehicle was giving him trouble. He hadn't been behind the wheel of anything in twelve years and other than a van, he'd never driven anything so big. Controlling the speed was difficult, primarily because of his damaged right foot. Making matters worse, the gauges on the dashboard were all new and different from a dozen years ago.

He cruised along the highway at forty-five miles per hour, sometimes letting it edge down to thirty-five. Passing cars were honking furiously at him. They'd gone roughly five miles when they saw a sign for a rest stop ahead, but when they got to it there was another sign saying that it was closed for renovation. Below it was a sign indicating that the next rest stop was twenty-five miles away.

The one thing Juliet had on her mind was getting her hands on a phone. If she couldn't find someone to let her borrow their phone, despite the fact that she had no money, she knew she could call her brother collect, if she could find a pay phone.

Trevor used the head start to try and come up with a Plan B. "This truck is too easy to spot with the smiling monks and all the berries. When we get to the next truck stop, we'll have to find another one."

"Meaning we'll have to steal one," said Juliet.

Trevor smirked. "Got any other suggestions. You can't just go up to a trucker and ask him if we can *borrow* his vehicle." Trevor's voice tinged with sarcasm. "Look, most truckers sleep or take a nap when they stop. We'll find one and pull the switch, hopefully without hurting anyone."

"How will you do it?"

"Let me worry about that."

"Will you promise you won't hurt anyone?"

"I'll try not to, but if he resists…"

"I don't want to hear about it."

"Then change the subject."

She hesitated for a few seconds. "How do you know about these things?" She asked the question even though she sort of knew the answer based on what Damian told her. She wanted to hear what Trevor said.

"What things?"

"Stealing."

"I had problems when I was a kid and I did some stupid stuff, bad stuff."

At least he's honest.

"But I've changed. I try to be a good person. That's how I've been ever since I got stuck here." He caught himself. "Wait a minute. I'm not 'here' anymore. I'm not 'there anymore. I'm out."

He pounded on the steering wheel with both hands and screamed, "I'm free! I never thought it would happen. Damian, we're free! Freeeeee!"

Then, Trevor burst into tears.

Juliet reached out and touched his hand with hers. She realized that she had misjudged him. She sincerely hoped that he would find his brother and be able to lead a normal life.

She turned around and looked at Damian. Unlike Trevor, he looked concerned.

"Damian, what's wrong?"

"Maybe this wasn't the right thing to do, Juliet. Maybe I should have stayed."

"No," she stated emphatically. "You did the right thing. Getting out will be your salvation. It'll be okay, Damian. You have to trust me."

Damian continued staring at her. He was getting more terrified of being outside of the reserve. And he couldn't get used to being in a truck. He wished he could get out and walk. He wished he could go back to Cassoulet Reserve and forget he'd ever left.

He missed his Uncle Pete.

He missed his life.

He was questioning his decision to leave.

CHAPTER

25

Vircuzi hesitated for several seconds to consider his choices. He turned to his computer and typed in a code. Within seconds a file appeared with the simple word:

Gigante

He double-clicked it and the file opened. There was a world-wide map, and at a dozen places there were markings. He clicked the one that said Cassoulet Reserve in the United States and hundreds of names of giants came up with their dates of birth and death. The most recent passing was four years ago and had the number 619 next to it. It was Damian's mother. Further down, there was another list, much shorter, with the names of the last surviving giants in the world.

The last number was 647.

He considered the number for a moment. He acknowledged to himself how detailed and thorough the records were. The monks were required to email him whenever a giant was born or died. Since the day seventeen years ago that 647 was born, thirty-seven giants had passed.

He clicked another file labeled Mont Blanc and found another list consisting of more than three thousand numbers accompanied first by their date of birth, and second, their date of death. The oldest went back to 1513 and had been recorded in cursive by monks from long ago.

He clicked open a third file labeled Mount Kilimanjaro and looked at a smaller list of giant's numbers, birth and death days.

As far as he was concerned, the long-standing giant problem the church had was over. The giants living in America were considered to be the last remaining giants in the world. They had never made a peep. He remembered the tales of giants escaping from Mont Blanc and Mount Kilimanjaro in the past when the monks tried to be more humane. They would have to be hunted down and killed. That's when the Knights Templars were first utilized.

He knew that type of action was easier in the past because there was nowhere for a giant on the loose to run to. The wide-open spaces of yesteryear were gone. If a giant escaped now, he would wreak havoc wherever he went. And if he were caught by the wrong people, it would be disastrous for the Church.

Archbishop Vircuzi sighed. He wished these last American giants were dead and he could concentrate on other things. There had been discussion in The

Vatican by younger clerics about doing just that, but it had gotten nowhere.

The pope said no.

"We will see it through until the end," said the pontiff. "We are not killers. We have treated the giants as humanely as possible for centuries, and we will continue to do so until the last one leaves us."

Archbishop Vircuzi sat stoically in his seat as his mind pondered one question:

Should he change his mind about giving Sulpience the order to kill all the giants without the blessing of the pope?

He knew that sometimes, what we don't know wouldn't hurt us.

Why should the pope have to know?

He picked up the phone and called Albert Sulpience.

CHAPTER

26

Sulpience heard his muted ringtone, a simple old-fashioned telephone ring, go off. He preferred the old to the new. He was about to let the call go to voice mail, as he always did, because he disliked being caught off guard. But when he saw the number from Italy, he knew the call meant it had to do with the Catholic Church. His service was required.

Vircuzi.

He remembered Vircuzi as a sly dog who seemed nothing like a priest, let alone an Archbishop. He was more like a cutthroat businessman.

"Archbishop Vircusi," he said respectfully. "How are you?"

"Not good, Albert. I just received a message from the Abbot in charge of the monastery at Cassoulet

Reserve. We have a big problem over there. You are the only man I can turn to."

He told him all that he knew about the escape concluding with this proviso. "That this giant got out will be catastrophic to the Church if he isn't stopped."

"I understand."

"If you find him, eliminate him and whomever helped him."

"Understood. What about the giants and others still residing in the reserve?"

"I want them all eliminated. The captives too. It shouldn't be difficult. They're all in one place. They are all old. Do it by fire."

"Fire?" The order unsettled Sulpience. "The reserve is close to forty thousand acres. Isn't there a better way?"

"They're all in one section. I want to make it simple. You can't go into the reserve with guns blazing. The giants may have places to hide. I want everyone there to be destroyed. Make it sudden and swift. Can you do it, Albert?"

"Yes, Archbishop."

"Call the Abbot and have him go over what he knows, which isn't much, and keep me posted."

"Yes, Archbishop."

"Needless to say, if there are complications, you must disavow any connection with the Catholic Church. The Church and the pope must be protected at all costs."

"Of course."

"Goodbye."

As he dialed the number, Sulpience was already calculating the manpower he would need for the mission. Because of his position in The Department of Defense, he immediately requested and received seven Black Ops helicopters. Two would be going to Cassoulet Reserve to handle the giants and everyone else there, while the others would be cruising over the highways leading from the reserve looking for a truck.

We have two situations," Sulpience wrote in his notebook, a form of discipline he'd perfected when he was in military school.

Stopping the giant who has escaped and dealing with everyone he left behind. From my point of view, stopping him is the more important.

If he or the people he's with go public, and I'm certain they will try, it would be disastrous for the Church.

He grew more and more frustrated. He didn't know which way the truck carrying the giant would be heading, and he had no idea how many box trucks travelled along the highways. He didn't know if it would be on the back roads. He didn't know if the people with him had allies who would help them. He had to rely on pure instinct, and his instinct told him that the truck would be heading to New York City with the purpose of making an announcement to the media.

He hoped that he was right.

CHAPTER

27

Abbot Gassner was so concerned and shaken about the events of the last hour he thought he would have a heart attack. He called his assistant, Brother Terrence, who at thirty-four, was thirty-five years his junior, and instructed him to come directly to the gate by the eastern section where he was waiting.

Brother Terrence got to him within ten minutes. He observed an ashen Gassner.

"We have a possibly insurmountable problem. A giant has escaped."

Brother Terrence looked alarmed, but said nothing. "Which one?"

"I'm assuming that it's six-forty-seven."

"His name is Damian."

"To me he's six-forty-seven. He has two regular-sized people with him. I don't know who they are. None of them are young enough or strong enough to climb down a mountain."

"What about Trevor?"

"With his crippled foot?"

"Damian could've carried him."

Gassner pondered the idea, then said, "It could be him. I hope it's not because I'm waiting for him now. Whoever it was stole one of our trucks. Lord knows where they're headed. If they get to a phone, it will expose what we've been doing."

"Could this possibly be a good thing, Abbot?"

Gassner stared at him with daggers in his eyes. "Are you insane?"

"It's simply that..." He hesitated.

"What? Out with it."

"Perhaps we could use this opportunity to end the secrecy."

"Don't be ridiculous."

"To come out with the news, with the truth. It's been so long. The world has grown up."

"The Vatican has given us a mandate to protect the giants."

"Did it ever occur to you that The Vatican might be wrong?" The remark unsettled Gassner. "Revealing that we have eleven giants and that giants once were plentiful might be just what the Church needs to uplift its image."

"That's heresy. We have been given a task, which we've maintained. There will be no more discussion of this."

"With you."

"With me?"

"Most of the other monks feel the way I do."

The remark shocked Abbot Gassner. "I don't believe you."

"We've wanted to go public for years. Now is the right time. A giant escaped. It's a sign from God."

"Never. Not on my watch. And I warn you, this kind of talk is very dangerous."

"I disagree," Brother Terrence said firmly. "It's time to tell the truth,"

"If you don't want to be transferred to our retreat house in the mountains of northern Canada where a warm day is fifteen below zero, you'd better mind your words."

Brother Terrence acknowledged the threat with cool silence.

The abbot knew that the young monk was right, but he couldn't let him know that he agreed. No good could come from it. Before the burden of the giants could be over for him, he would have to wait out their deaths. He knew that, other than 647, they were all in their thirties with the exception of 634, which was Martin's number, and he also knew that giants rarely lived past forty.

The Vatican always got what it wanted. Just talking to Archbishop Vircuzi sent a chill up Gassner's spine. If he didn't capitulate, *he* would be the one banished to northern Canada or some other godforsaken locale. He liked living in the monastery. The countryside was beautiful, as were the mountains. It was peaceful. Serene. And he felt he was doing God's work by running retreats and growing the jams and jellies. If he honestly acknowledged it, maintaining the giants was something he rarely thought about.

But today was different. His thoughts turned to 647. At seventeen, he would have many years of life ahead of him. He could live for another twenty years or more. Abbot Gassner felt ashamed to be thinking what went through his mind.

But he knew that life, his life, would be better if 647 were gone.

His thoughts turned back to Albert Sulpience.

The man had come through for him three times during his tenure at Cassoulet reserve when people tried to escape. He knew the man was capable. He'd heard that Albert had come through for the Church on three other occasions over the years. The first time to capture a renegade priest threatening to reveal the truth about exorcisms, the second time a nun with a big mouth who challenged doctrine about the birth of Christ and the third time, one year ago, when a miracle credited to a candidate for sainthood had proven not to have happened.

Abbot Gassner tried to process the fact that it would be over soon if Damian went public. His hands were shaking.

Then his phone rang. He glanced at the Caller ID. There was none.

"Hello?" he said nervously.

"This is Albert Sulpience. So, abbot, one of your giants has escaped?"

Gassner cupped the phone and turned to Brother Terrence. "It's the Templar. You should hear this." He put the call on speaker.

"That is correct."

"What do you know so far?" asked Sulpience.

"Not much. He's riding in one of our trucks."

"Is it a truck without advertising or does it have anything on it identifying your products?"

"There are drawings of two smiling monks surrounded by berries on each side and on the top is one jolly-looking monk. And, of course, there is our logo."

"Who's driving him?"

"I don't know."

"How big is the giant?"

Gassner looked at Brother Terrence who mouthed the words, "Fifteen or sixteen feet."

"Fifteen or sixteen feet."

"That's helpful. It stands to reason that they'll be driving on a highway. North is Canada and I doubt they'll be going there because they'll have to go through the border. South is New York City, which may be better in the event they want to make some kind of statement to the public, to the media. They'll want to expose the Church."

"Yes."

"No one will believe them."

"Why do you say that?" Gassner felt a moment of relief.

"I've already personally contacted the news directors of all major networks warning them of such a call. National security."

Abbot Gassner perked up as if he were a naïve child. "You can do *that*?"

"Let's just say I have friends in very high places. Besides, everyone knows that giants don't exist." He chuckled. "Whoever calls in about the giant will be shut down by the media. They may have your giant, but they have to get him somewhere in public and right now they're in the middle of nowhere. I've received my orders from the Archbishop."

"You have to kill them."

"Yes."

Gassner glanced at Brother Terrence. "What if you can't find him, Mister Sulpience?"

"I choose to be positive, not negative."

"Yes, but what if he gets away and makes an announcement to the media? It could happen."

"Do you have an alternate plan, Abbot Gassner?"

"Mister Sulpience, I only found out about the escape a short time ago. I have no other plans

"You're new to this."

"To say the least. I am a Catholic monk, not a killer."

"I am a Knight Templar, an advocate of the Catholic Church. My job is to protect it and the pope at all costs. How many giants are there left?"

Gassner glanced at Brother Terrence.

"Eleven."

"Eleven."

"And how many human-sized prisoners are there?"

"I don't recall offhand. Possibly fifteen. Why?"

"They will have to be eliminated too."

Gassner looked at Brother Terrence.

"My men will handle the job, obviously," said Sulpience.

"Ask him when that will be," said Brother Terrence.

"When will you do it?"

"Today. I have two helicopters on their way to you. I have a question. Do you have any idea where the giant who escaped and his associates might be heading?"

"No. What if you can't find him? What if he manages to escape and go public?"

Sulpience hesitated, then said, "Then the Catholic Church will have a lot of explaining to do."

Abbot Gassner felt a pain in his chest.

"I'm concentrating my efforts on the highways going north and south," said Sulpience. "When my men arrive, stay out of their way."

"How will they kill them?"

"By fire."

The answer stunned Gassner. "Fire? This is a nature reserve. You can't destroy thirty-seven thousand acres."

"We'll concentrate on the eastern section. I'm acting on the orders of the Archbishop. I'm hanging up. God willing, I have a giant to find."

Gassner felt faint. His heart was pounding fast again. Nevertheless, he took several deep breaths, then turned to Brother Terrence.

"I never thought it would come to this," said Gassner.

Then a loud pounding noise came from the other side of the wall.

Gassner and Brother Terrence looked at each other cautiously.

"Trevor?" Gassner shouted. "Is that you, Trevor? This is Abbot Gassner."

"That is not Trevor," said Brother Terrence.

"Then who is it?"

"Obviously, one of the giants."

Abbot Gassner looked up at the wall, shaking.

CHAPTER

28

They were on the highway for almost thirty minutes hoping to see a sign for a rest stop.

"Where is it?" said Juliet, banging her hands against the dashboard. "The sign said twenty-five miles. If you weren't going so slow, we'd be there by now."

Trevor ignored her remark.

She continued. "We have to assume that by now they'll realize somebody stole their truck. They've probably already called the police."

"I doubt it. If they did and the cops were looking for us and they found us, they would find Damian. They wouldn't want that to happen."

Juliet nodded. "So that means we're okay in this truck."

"No. Being in this thing makes me nervous."

"Why?"

"Because if somebody is looking for us, they'll be looking for a truck with smiling monks and berries all over it. We've got to get rid of it."

Juliet spotted a sign up ahead:

Rest Stop 3 Miles.

"We're coming to a rest stop. Thank God!"

"Good. Okay, be prepared to move fast."

"Move where?"

"Into another truck. Let's hope there's one here and that it's big enough to hold Damian."

"Wait," said Juliet. "Shouldn't our first priority be to get a phone? So,I can call my brother and tell him I'm alright and then I should call the media and someone can come and get us?"

"No," said Trevor. "We have to get out of this truck first."

"But... "

"First we dump the truck, then we'll find you a phone," he said adamantly.

Juliet turned around and looked at Damian. "What do you think we should do, Damian?"

"I think Trevor is right. If you can make,,, your calls, what good will it be if they spot the truck and capture us?"

Juliet pondered what he said. "Okay. Makes sense. Trevor, we'll try to get a truck.'

As they pulled into the truck area Trevor noticed a tractor trailer that would fit Damian perfectly with plenty of extra room, provided it were empty. Trevor pulled up alongside it and noticed the driver eating a sandwich. There were no markings of any kind to indicate the load he was carrying.

"Juliet, find out what he's carrying," Trevor asked.

Juliet got out of the truck and stretched, pretending that her legs were sore from sitting. She casually walked over to the trucker's window.

"Hi!"

"Hey there." He had a scraggly beard and appeared to be in his early thirties.

"Been on the road long?" she asked.

"Four hours. I always stop every four hours to stretch my legs."

"I know what you mean. What are you carrying?"

"Shrimp and lobster," he replied. "By the way, I love them jams and jellies you make." He gestured to the truck. My favorite is boysenberry."

"Oh. Yeah. They're great."

"Where you headed?" he asked.

"Uh, New York City."

"Philadelphia."

"Ah. Okay. Well, later."

She walked around to Trevor and said, "No go. Fish. There aren't any other trucks here. I think I should go inside and try to find a phone."

"Not yet. Get back in the truck."

"Why?"

"A police car just entered the lot."

She turned her head and saw the police cruiser. "So? We didn't do anything wrong?"

She looked again and saw the police car coming up the entrance ramp.

"I want to get out of here," said Trevor nervously. "Get in!"

Juliet climbed inside and shut the door. "Are you gonna be this paranoid all the time?"

"Yes. The last time I was outside of the reserve I was hiding from cops."

Suddenly, the police car came to a stop in front of the concessions building, about forty yards away. The one riding shotgun got out and went inside.

"They're stopping for food," Juliet snapped. She perked up. "And look there?" Juliet pointed at another semi pulling into the lot. "Let's wait so I can check his load."

"Those cops are making me nervous. Let's try at the next rest stop."

"That could be thirty-five miles away. You said we don't have a lot of gas."

Suddenly, another semi pulled into the lot. She and Trevor both watched the truck as the driver maneuvered it into a parking space twenty feet away. He got out, did a few stretches and headed to the Port-o-Potty nearby.

"Should I go check out his load?" asked Juliet.

"No," said Trevor. "I'll do it. I need to stretch my legs. He slid out of the truck. Keep your fingers crossed."

The instant he was gone Juliet turned and looked at Damian. "I'm so happy for you. Freedom! Damian, you never have to go back to that horrible place."

"I hope not," he said softly.

"Damian, you are free! It's probably hard to get used to, but it will be the most amazing thing. Trust me."

He hesitated, and then said, "Okay."

Trevor made his way to the rear of the truck, opened the door and saw that it was filled to the brim with stereo speakers. He turned to Juliet, who was watching him from the window, and shook his head no.

Trevor walked up to the Port-o-Potty the driver was in and waited. Two minutes later the door opened and Trevor sucker-punched the guy in the mouth twice, knocking him out. He grabbed his wallet, took out all the cash and one credit card. The trucker's iPhone was in his shirt pocket. Trevor lifted it, then moved his unconscious body back into the Port-o-Potty.

He made his way back to the truck and gave the phone to Juliet.

"Call your brother."

"Did the truck driver lend you his phone?" said Juliet.

Trevor glared at her. "Just dial your brother."

"Did you hurt him?"

"He'll be all right. Dial!"

She quickly typed in Greg's number.

Trevor leaned back towards Damian and said, "How you doin' Damian?"

"I keep thinking this is a mistake," said the giant.

"The only mistake was you and I not doing it before."

"I don't know," said Damian. "I just don't know."

"Let's get outa here!" said Trevor as he turned the ignition key.

CHAPTER

29

Martin spoke first, his voice thundering through the wall. "Can ya hear me?"

"Yes." Gassner turned to Brother Terrence. "That's not Trevor."

"I can't hear you," Martin thundered again. "Speak up."

"Try the intercom, abbot," said Brother Terrence.

Gassner moved to the intercom. "Can you hear me now?"

"Yes. Bloody barely."

Gassner turned to Brother Terrence. "He does have an English accent."

"Most of them do."

Martin crouched down onto his knees and put his face close to the intercom. "Who called Trevor?"

"I did. Who is this?"

"Who are *you*?"

"Abbot Gassner."

"Are you in charge?"

"Yes."

"So, you don't know who I am."

"How could I? I can't see you."

"My name is Martin."

"You're one of the giants?"

"Obviously. Although you probably refer to me as a number. Number 634 to be specific."

"Where's Trevor? I need to talk to Trevor."

"He's gone."

"Did he leave with six-forty-seven, I mean, Damian?" asked the abbot.

"Yes."

"Oh my God!" The realization that Trevor had gotten out devastated him. He turned to Brother Terrence. "It's all going to come crashing down."

"Have you ever talked to a giant before?" asked Martin.

"No."

"I've never talked to a monk. What is it like to talk to a giant?"

"Odd."

"Yeah. So, you're the boss. I'm the boss too. In here."

"I didn't know you had such a thing."

"We have to maintain order."

"There were three sets of footprints," said Gassner, changing the subject. "Who does the third belong to?"

"The girl."

"The girl?" Gassner was taken aback. "What girl?" he asked Brother Terrence.

"The new girl," said Martin. "Her name is Juliet."

"Wait. What do you mean 'new' girl?"

"She survived the plane crash."

Gassner sighed. "So, there *was* a crash." To Brother Terrence he said, "Trevor lied to me." His mind was spinning. "When?"

"Four or five days ago."

"How could she have found a way out?"

"It wasn't her," said Martin. "It was Damian. Six-forty-seven, as you call him. He found the hole in the mountain."

"A hole?"

"He kept it secret. He found it two years ago. That's all I know. What is it like, abbot?"

"What is what like?"

"To talk to a giant. I'd really like to know?"

"I'd heard that the giants could speak well, but I had no idea you would be so articulate. How did that happen?"

"I'd have thought you would've known our history. What did you want Trevor for?"

"To find out where they're going. Do you know?"

"No. Trevor wanted the girl for himself. We needed a cook. We found her first in our territory. Damian broke the rules."

"What rules?"

"He came into my territory. You think we can live in here without rules? It's how we keep order. We've always had rules."

"Are they going to tell what's gone on here all these years?"

"I don't know. I hope so. If you were kept against your will for your entire life wouldn't you want people to know?"

Gassner squirmed. "We had our reasons."

"I'm sure you did."

"They were motivated by a greater good."

"What good was that, abbot?" said Martin.

"I'm not going to debate you on that right now. This is bad. This is so terribly bad. Where are they going?"

"There's only one place that I can figure Damian wants to go."

With great anticipation, Gassner asked, "Where?"

"To Mont Blanc in France."

"He knows about Mont Blanc?"

"We all do. From the oral history."

Gassner looked at Brother Terrence as if to say, "They had an oral history?"

Brother Terrence nodded.

"Why would Damian want to go to Mont Blanc?" asked Gassner.

"He thinks there are giants there."

"The giants of Mont Blanc are all dead."

"What?" The news stunned Martin.

"Wiped out by disease years ago. How would he expect to get there?"

"I don't know. I haven't spent much time thinking about it. I never thought this day would come. It's very overwhelming."

"What day is that?" asked Gassner. "That a giant would escape?"

"No. That I would meet the man who kept me imprisoned here for my entire life."

"How old are you?"

"Twenty-six."

"I'm sorry, but I was following orders from The Vatican. Do you know what The Vatican is?"

"Of course. That's where the Pope lives. He's in Rome. Vatican City. When we weren't busy trying to survive, we would talk. One of us learned something from an abnormal and would share it. We all have friends with the abnormals. That's how we learned. What are you going to do about this problem?"

"At the moment, I don't know," said Gassner.

"If they make it, you know they'll tell the world about what's gone on here."

"I can't even imagine what the consequences would be if this got out to the public." He stared off for several seconds, looked upwards to the heavens and felt lost.

"Abbot Gassner?" said Brother Terrence. "Let's bring it to an end now before the soldiers come and kill everyone." Abbot Gassner turned towards his young assistant. "I... I... ", then he nodded his head in agreement.

Brother Terrence spoke into the Intercom. "Martin, my name is Brother Terrence. All of the monks here at St. Albans have wanted to free you and the others for years, but until today we never had the chance. What you need to know is that men are coming to kill you. All of you. Giants and regular people alike. They're going to do it by fire. We can't stop them. If you want to die, remain in the reserve. If you want to live, come out and let us help you."

What he said stunned Martin. "How will we get out?"

"The regular-sized people will exit through the door where you are now. As for the giants, we'll knock down the wall around the door. Is there a way that you can gather all the giants and the other people in one place?"

"I can do that," said Martin.

"Please do it right now."

"And where will we go?"

"I can't say yet, but for the time being we can put you all in our warehouse."

"What's a warehouse?"

"A building."

"What's a building?"

"Someplace you'll be safe. I want to get you out of the reserve so you'll be safe."

"So, we can all be killed."

"No. We don't have time to argue. If you want to live, get all the normal-sized people in the reserve together. Bring them here and I'll let them out. They can stay in the retreat house for the time being. We'll worry about reuniting them with their families later."

"They're all old men and women."

"Some will have families who will welcome them back."

"All they'll have is each other and most of them don't get along."

"I'm sorry to hear that," said Brother Terrence.

"As am I," said Gassner.

"Are you? I doubt it." Martin was hesitant. "I'll agree to this on one condition."

"Yes."

"I want the abbot to come in here and wait for them with me."

The statement caught Gassner off guard. "I would like to, but there are things I have to do to prepare."

Martin was suspicious by nature, but he felt it in his gut that the brother named Terrence was telling the truth.

"I need some guarantee that whoever's coming to kill us *won't*," Martin said. "Have the Abbot come inside. I'll walk out of here with him. If you don't, I'll tell everyone to hide and there are many places where we can hide. Whoever is coming won't be able to find us. Maybe we won't come out until Damian goes public."

"If he makes it," snapped Gassner.

"Yes. If he makes it, but with the head start he has, he might. And then what will happen to you? If he can tell the world about this place, the world will come here and then we'll come out with a lot to say. But if you come in here now and talk to the giants and apologize, we'll go peacefully."

Gassner hesitated. He looked at Brother Terrence, not quite sure what to do.

"Go in," said Brother Terrence.

"I can't. I'm afraid."

Brother Terrence looked at Gassner. "Martin, Abbot Gassner is an elderly man. The events of the last hour have taken their toll on him."

"I don't bloody care."

"Martin, I want Damian to go public. I hope he goes public. I want him to tell the world about this place, but the men who are coming to kill you will be here soon. I urge you to get the giants and everyone else out now."

"I want the Abbot to come inside and apologize for this travesty, then we'll all come out."

Brother Terrence looked at Abbot Gassner who returned the look, not quite sure what to do.

"He doesn't know what I look like," said Gassner. "Pretend your me."

"I can't do that, Abbot."

"I'm ordering you to do it, Brother Terrence."

Martin pounded on the wall three more times. "Are you coming?"

"Tell him yes," said Brother Terrence.

Brother Terrence reached for the keys on his belt, found the three that opened the door and did so.

"You don't know what you're doing," said Abbot Gassner.

"Yes, I do. It's coming to an end. Give me your phone."

Feeling defeated and tired, the old abbot weakly handed the younger brother his iPhone.

"Go in now," said Brother Terrence. "And maybe he won't hurt you." He gestured to the open door.

Abbot Gassner's heart was still beating ferociously. A part of him wanted to die. The old man nodded yes and walked up to the open door. He looked as if he'd aged ten years. "We have to stop the Templar's men from coming. You have to call his superior. His name is Vircuzi. He's an Archbishop."

"Does he speak for the Pope?" asked Brother Terrence.

"Yes."

"Get him on the phone. Tell him to cancel the plan to kill the giants. When he asks you why, tell him that they're being let out and there's no need to."

"He'll want an explanation."

"Tell him the truth. That the monks of St. Albans revolted against me."

"Is he coming?" said Martin.

"It's time," said Brother Terrence. He opened the door. Abbot Gassner, breathing hard and fast, entered the reserve. He looked back at Terrence.

"You must protect the Church. I beg you."

Brother Terrence said nothing and closed the door.

Like a beaten animal, Abbot Gassner stepped into the reserve. He heard the door close and lock behind him. He looked up and saw his first giant staring down at him.

Martin crouched down.

"I didn't think you would have the courage to come in," said Martin. "What's it like, Abbot?"

"What is what like?"

"Having no power. Over anyone."

Martin stood up, cupped his hands to his mouth and then let loose with a cacophonous roar four times. It was a call to all giants to alert them that one of them needed help. It was rarely used, so when any of them heard it, they dropped whatever they were doing and headed to the sound.

Then in an almost Morse Code staccato, he roared out about a dozen other noises which translated to the abnormals to meet at the gate.

Throughout the reserve the messages resonated, and each giant and abnormal began making their way to the entrance, even Pete. He knew something was up, but he didn't know if it was good or bad. For a moment he wondered if something had gone wrong with Damian's escape plan.

Martin crouched down and brought himself to eye level with Abbot Gassner.

"I don't feel well," said the Abbot. "I feel like I'm having a heart attack."

"Then you'll die. We don't have doctors in here."

CHAPTER

30

Juliet took the phone and punched in her brother's number. Greg answered after the first ring.

"Greg, it's me."

He almost fell over. "Where are you, Juliet?"

"You have to listen. I'm okay. You're not gonna believe what happened to me or where I am, but you've got to promise me you won't think I'm crazy. Do you promise?"

"Yes."

"The plane I was on crashed."

"That's what I thought happened."

"I was the only one who survived. I was rescued by... this is the part you have to believe, Greg. I was rescued by a giant."

"What?"

Giants again?

"I'm not kidding. He's like three times my size and lives with his uncle, who's also a giant, and they live in a cave in a place where other giants live. It's a forest."

"Cassoulet Reserve? By Hammerhead Mountain?"

Juliet was shocked. "Yes. How did you know? Anyway, we became friends. His name's Damian."

She was carrying on so strongly that Greg wondered if she'd had a concussion from the plane crash, but he remembered everything that Edward Purdell had told him.

"The giants have been held prisoner in the reserve for like a hundred-and-fifty years by the Catholic Church," she continued. "I know that sounds insane, but it's true."

"Juliet..."

"And they're guarded by a bunch of monks. They live in a monastery on the other side of the reserve. They make jellies and jams."

"Juliet... "

"I'm leaving lots of stuff out, but Damian found a way to escape. He needed me to help, so we're free now. What I need you to do is contact the media because Damian is going to tell everything."

"Which media?"

"All of them. Television, radio, newspaper... "

"How do I do that? I'm a high school junior from Denver who plays French horn in the school band."

"Maybe you're right." She thought for a few seconds. "Just Google CNN. There will be an 800 number. Ask for the news desk and tell them your sister's been held prisoner by a bunch of monks and that she's going to expose them. She'll be with a giant who has escaped and is going to tell the world."

"Dude, take a breath."

Juliet was concerned. "I can tell from that tone that you don't believe me."

"Juliet, I believe you."

"You do?"

He does?

"Yes. I'm just happy you're all right. Where are you?"

"At a rest stop on the highway somewhere in upstate New York. I'm not sure exactly where we are. All I know is that we're heading south and we're coming to New York."

"Why all the way down here?"

"We want to make the announcement in the capital of the world. What you can't do is call the police because they'll think Damian's some kind of giant monster, but he isn't, and I know I'm rambling. I'm scared that we're gonna get caught before we can tell the truth about what's happened. Anyway, I just wanted you to know that I'm fine. We're gonna try and switch trucks because the one we're in is pretty recognizable. Do you believe me? Please say that you believe me."

"Yes! This is so bizarre that you mentioned giants. When I was trying to look for you, a guy was referred to me. His name is Edward Purdell. He conducts tours around Cassoulet reserve. I hired him and, well, he brought up giants living in the reserve. I thought he was crazy."

"What did he say?"

"That monks keep guard.”

“Oh my God! He knows. We have an ally.”

“He said pretty much everything you said."

"And he lives around here?"

"Yes. I flew up there yesterday to look for you in the reserve.”

“You were here? Oh my God!”

“We flew over and over the trees trying to find your plane, but we saw nothing."

“I don't believe it, Greg. I heard your plane. I kept screaming for help, but I was too far away. You need to call this man and tell him where I am. He can help us. Better yet, give me his phone number. I'll call him.”

“Hold on. I threw it away.” He went to the trashcan near the bed and saw the brochure the concierge had given him. He scooped it up and read the number to Juliet.

“Greg, you call him first, and then I'll call him. He's just the person we need to help us.”

“I haven't called dad yet,” he said.

“Good. Don't until you and I are together. He won't be able to do anything. Besides, he's got enough problems with a flooded house. Oh Greg, if Damian didn't find a way out, I would've had to stay there forever. I never would have seen you again."

Suddenly, the phone cut off.

"Shit!" Juliet screamed. "Greg? Greg?"

"Juliet? Juliet! Damn!"

One second later Greg called Edward Purdell and told him about the phone call from his sister.

"She's actually *with* a *giant*?" asked Edward.

"Yes."

"Have her call me right away. This is incredible information. I've waited my entire life for this."

"She doesn't have a phone. She has to borrow somebody's."

"Very well. I'll wait right here."

"Thanks."

"Greg?"

"Yeah?"

"Do you believe me now?"

"Yes."

"I'll wait for your sister's call."

Edward's mind was already working. He felt that this was a gift from God. He had given up so many times over the years of ever proving what he knew to be true about giants. He'd become so disillusioned that he almost stopped believing what he knew was even true.

But now, if the sister of Greg Pine and the giant were with him, he could finally enact a plan he'd gone over hundreds of times in his head.

He stared at his iPhone, waiting for Juliet to call. He checked his contact list and found the name of a man he had never met, but to whom he felt as close as if they were brothers. They talked several times a year by Skype and emailed each other periodically to exchange new information about giants. Not that there was much. But the two men had formed a bond and now, finally, their mutual obsession would finally be resolved. He wanted to call him, but decided to wait until he had seen the giant in person.

He stared at his name on his contact list.

Henri Marteen.

As for Greg, he made a call too. The phone rang three times then the person picked up.

"Parterra."

"Chief Parterra, I'm the guy who called you a few days ago about my sister being in a plane crash? By Hammerhead Mountain?"

Parterra remembered. "Yes. What can I do for you?"

"I thought she was missing, but she's not. I just talked to her. She's in trouble. I know this will sound crazy, but she's with a giant."

"A giant?"

Parterra immediately remembered the rumors he'd heard about monsters being in Cassoulet Reserve since he was a little boy, giants in particular.

"How do you know she's with a giant?"

"Because they escaped. They stole one of the monks' trucks and they're driving south, heading to New York City."

"Hold on. Backtrack a little. Why are you calling me? What am I supposed to do, assuming what you say is true?"

"I called because you're the only person I know that could help. I mean, you are the Chief of Police."

Parterra tried to think of what he could do, assuming Greg Pine was telling him the truth.

"Tell you what," he said. "This sounds ridiculous, but as a favor to you, I'll take a drive over to the abbey and see what's going on. Okay?"

"Okay."

Parterra got into his cruiser and headed over. That Greg Pine's sister was alive and had escaped intrigued him, but even more so, as a boy he had latched on to the stories about Cassoulet Reserve having giants in it. He and his friends would climb Hammerhead Mountain and call out to the giants who never returned their greetings. He stopped believing they were there when he was twelve, when his older brother, whom he idolized, said to him, "Only an idiot believes in giants."

That was the day he put the notion out of his mind.

CHAPTER

31

Brother Terrence called Brother Timothy as soon as Gassner entered the reserve.

"We need to work fast. First, we have to get the giants and the others out of the reserve. Once that happens, we need to call the media. I want you to do that Timothy."

"Yes, brother, but I should tell you that I never watch television. Once in a while I listen to the radio. I don't even watch the news. I rely strictly on the newspaper for my information."

"Doesn't matter. I want you to call the news director at the Public Television station. His name is Dan Frigoli."

"Yes, brother."

"Don't call him until I tell you to. When I give you the word, tell him to get a news crew over here. Tell him it'll be the biggest story of the station's existence. Tell him he's the only one we're contacting."

"What do I say when he asks what the story is?"

Terrence considered the question. "Ask him if believes in giants. Wait for his response, and then tell him the truth."

"What if he doesn't believe me?"

"You're a monk at St. Alban's Retreat House. Monks don't lie."

Timothy nodded yes. "Shouldn't I call the other stations? There are two more."

"Dan Frigoli made a retreat here last year, which means he's catholic. I think he came reluctantly, his wife made him, but he might actually believe you. Besides, I don't want to scare the giants. One news crew will be enough."

"Could a giant really be scared of anything?"

"As soon as they step outside this wall, they'll see things they never have. The warehouse. The factory. Cars. Trucks. Civilization. We'll see how they handle it."

Brother Terrence turned to Brother Simon, who had just approached him. "We have to move quickly. Go to the plant and get the forklift."

"Forklift, brother?"

"We're going to make an exit for the giants."

"We're knocking down the wall with a forklift?"

"Not the wall itself. The area by the door."

Brother Simon glanced at the entrance. "Do you think it'll work?"

"Forklifts are all we've got. In fact, ask Brother Gary to go with you and bring two."

"Whatever you say." Brother Simon smiled and said, "Be right back."

Phone in hand, Brother Terrence pressed Vircuzi's number. He waited anxiously.

This time he answered the call himself.

"Archbishop Vircuzi."

"My name is Brother Terrence. I'm the personal assistant to Abbot Gassner at Saint Alban's Monastery in the States."

"Yes?" Vircuzi said suspiciously. "I just spoke to him."

"I know. I was listening in on your conversation. We have a situation here."

"Do you and I have a situation or do *I* have one?"

"I'd say The Roman Catholic Church has a situation."

Vircuzi stood up and began pacing. "Get to it."

"The monks serving the church under Abbot Gassner have rebelled against him. We refuse to allow the giants and the people we've kept imprisoned in the reserve to die. We know of your plans to have them killed. We're going to release them all."

"I see." Vircuzi felt sweat forming around his neck.

"I advise you to call off your men, Archbishop. We'll be holding a press conference within the next hour.

We're going to announce what the Church has done. We're going to present the giants to the world. We're going to let any of the people imprisoned in there talk if they want to."

Vircuzi was outraged, but his gut told him not to show it. "The Church must be protected at all costs."

"Abbot Gassner said the same thing. One question: why?"

"Think of the consequences."

"The consequences are that the world will finally learn about its past. The giants are part of that past. It's like concealing the fact that there were dinosaurs."

"Listen to reason, I beg you."

"No. I know that the Templar has sent men here to kill the giants. Instruct him to call it off."

"All I'm asking is that you leave The Pope out of this mess. He must not be connected to this."

"Did he know about the giants?"

"Yes, but he and those before him insisted that we keep them alive."

The remark resonated with Brother Terrence.

"Put the blame on me," said Vircuzi. "I accept full responsibility."

"Call the Templar and tell him it's over."

"Tell the media that a renegade branch of the Roman Catholic Church was responsible. And as I said, blame me. Do I have your word?"

"Yes."

"Very well."

The Escape of Giant 647

Brother Terrence heard Vircuzi disconnect him. Vircuzi steamed as he tried to organize his thoughts and figure out what to do. He never anticipated the rebellion of the monks.

Monks don't rebel. They never rebel.

CHAPTER

32

Juliet was so excited she could hardly breathe.

"I talked to my brother," Juliet said to Trevor and Damian. "He gave me the number of a guy who might be able to help us. I couldn't call him because the phone went dead. We have to find another one."

She got out of the truck. "I'll be back."

There were seven cars parked in the lot outside of the buildings. Two families were seated at picnic tables. They both had small children. She went inside to look for someone young who she could ask to borrow their phone.

She spotted a young couple, one of whom was talking on a smart phone and approached them.

"Hi. My cell phone just died. Could I possibly borrow one of yours?"

The girl smiled and said "Sure." She handed Juliet the phone.

"Thank you so much."

Juliet put in Edward Purdell's number. He answered it immediately. "Purdell."

"Mister Purdell, this is Juliet Pine. You spoke to my brother about the giants?"

"Yes. Do you actually have one with you?"

"Yes."

"I'll be damned! How do you have him contained? Unconscious and tied up?"

"No! He's in the back of a truck."

"Is he not restrained?"

"No."

"Aren't you afraid he'll hurt you or run away?"

"No. Why would he run away? He's the one who came up with the plan to escape."

"Wait. *He* came up with the plan?"

"Yes."

"I don't understand. How can he lead? How can he communicate with you?"

"He speaks perfect English. In fact, he speaks with a British accent."

"What?"

"Long story. He sounds just like you and me. He's educated. He has a fine mind. The only thing that makes him different from me or you is that he's so tall."

D. B Gilles

"Unbelievable! I thought he would be an ignorant lout."

"He's anything but. He wants to tell the world what the Catholic Church has done to his race."

"This goes beyond my wildest dreams. Where are you?"

"I'm not sure. On a highway. We're heading to New York City, but we're trying to get rid of the truck we're in because it's so noticeable."

"How many miles are you from the monastery?"

"I don't know. Maybe fifty or sixty, but I really don't know for sure."

"Can you ask someone what town you're in?"

Juliet turned to the girl. "Excuse me, what town is this rest stop in?"

"Jeffers."

"Thanks." Then to Edward, Juliet said, "Jeffers."

"You're only about thirty-five miles from where I am. You have to head back to where you came from. My place is only twelve miles from Hammerhead Mountain. Here's how to get to there."

CHAPTER

33

Albert Sulpience was in the front of an CH-53E Super Stallion helicopter heading upstate with his eyes glued to the highway on the ground looking for a caricature of a smiling monk. He had three other men also looking for the same thing, as were the men in the four other CH-53E Super Stallion on other highways.

Usually Sulpience was a positive man, but this assignment bothered him. He felt that there wasn't enough time for him to have even a remote chance of finding the truck.

Known for has fast and efficient work ethic, he was on his way out of his office before he even finished talking to Archbishop Vircuzi. He was picked up by a corporate helicopter on the rooftop of his office building within fifteen minutes and taken to JFK Airport where he boarded the CH-53E Super Stallion. All the while he was in motion, his brain worked overtime trying to come up with various scenarios of escape that the giant and his two companions might have cooked up.

He was direct with the men when he explained the mission.

"We're looking for a truck with a smiling monk on its roof. Inside the truck is a giant."

"Sir?" asked Lieutenant Gavin Bruce.

"A fifteen-to-sixteen-foot tall giant. This is not a joke."

"The giant is the target, sir?"

"Yes."

"Sir, are you serious about this mission? A giant? I mean... "

"Yes. Here's what you need to know. When we find him, he must first be subdued. We will eliminate him later. We can't take the chance that there will be witnesses. That is what we will do today. Understood?"

The three men all said, "Yes, sir." Sulpience instructed Gavin Bruce to contact the men on the other choppers with the same information.

Sulpience felt that whoever was driving would try to get a different truck, but he knew that would be difficult. He was certain they would need someone or some group of people helping them, but he didn't know who those people could be. He felt that he had a slim chance of spotting the truck with the smiling monk on the top. He was hoping that the giant would be uncomfortable in the back of the truck and would need to get out and stretch. He assumed that the three of them would have no money for gasoline or food and

270

that they might have to resort to robbery, probably at a truck stop. Every second he was in the air, the more probabilities and possibilities entered his mind.

He was certain that they would want media attention, which is why he called the presidents of all major news outlets warning them of a call about giants being imprisoned at a monastery in upstate New York. In no uncertain terms, he instructed them to ignore the call because of national security and under penalty of treason. He knew that the cynical New York media would sneer when they were told a giant wanted to go public anyway, but he still made the calls.

From JFK, the helicopter flew over the Bruckner Expressway (I-278), then on to the Hutchinson Parkway and north. He calculated that the fugitives' head start could work in his favor because they wouldn't be stopping anytime soon. They had a destination, but what was it? Or maybe they didn't have a destination and they were just winging it. He hoped that the person driving may not be entirely comfortable with the latest technology of the truck. He hoped that the truck might break down or run out of gas or have engine problems of some sort.

As he thought, he watched the highway. Seeing nothing resembling a smiling monk on top of all the various box trucks he saw, he began to wonder if he was wrong. Maybe they weren't going to New York. Maybe they were going to Albany. Albany wasn't considered a big city, but it was the capital of New York. Or maybe they were going to Buffalo or Canada. His mind raced and he began to consider what would happen if they actually found a way to make an announcement attacking the Church.

He was a Knight Templar by heredity. He could not fail the Church. He could not fail his family.

He reached for his walkie-talkie and contacted the chopper that was checking on the southbound lanes.

"Anything?"

"No sir. You see anything?"

"Nothing."

"Keep looking."

Sulpience looked down at the highway, wondering what would happen if he failed at finding the giant.

CHAPTER

34

Edward Purdell's directions were easy to follow until Trevor saw an interminable row of orange cones that led to a detour prior to the exit. There was a traffic jam that seemed endless and it was too late for him to back up, even if he knew how to maneuver the large truck.

What he didn't know was that the two smiling monks on top of the truck were there for anyone to see who was flying in a helicopter.

"This sucks," he said.

Juliet leaned out the window and observed the traffic jam. "There are hundreds of cars."

"And they're barely moving. We could be in this for an hour or longer."

Trevor looked at her and sighed, then turned around. "How you doing, Damian?"

"It's hot back here and I need to stretch."

"It's gonna be a while."

Juliet turned around and rubbed the back of Damian's head. Then she closed her eyes and tried to relax.

Trevor stared straight ahead.

As he waited his thoughts turned to the future. What would he do if his brother wasn't living in their house? Where would he go? What would he do for money? He was beginning to again rethink his decision to disappear.

Juliet was thinking about her future too. She was relieved that she had escaped from Cassoulet Reserve, but the thought of going on national television and exposing the Catholic Church for what they did to Damian and the other giants was daunting. And even though she had told Damian she would protect him, she wondered how she could do that? She would need help, more than help from her brother. She could call her father in Denver, but he was just a high school English teacher. He didn't have any clout.

Damian lay in the back of the truck pondering his decision to escape. In the short time he'd been free, he wasn't enjoying it. He again wondered if escaping was the right decision.

Fifty-two minutes later the traffic started to move.

Trevor was still ruminating about his future. He loved being free, such as it was. Everything had happened so fast, he hadn't had a moment's time to think about his next step. When would he leave Damian and Juliet? He had the money and credit card he took from the truck driver, which would cover his needs until he made it to his brother's house.

But then what?

When he got the idea of staying with his brother, he hadn't thought it through. What if indeed he had moved? Or what if he was married with kids or had a mother-in-law living with him? Or what if he were dead? He acknowledged the definite possibility that he might show up at night in case his brother no longer lived there.

But they were close. Connor would certainly take him in. He would help him get a new identity. Or was Juliet right? Maybe the cops would forgive him for the crimes he committed. Twelve years in the reserve was definitely a greater punishment than he would've gotten if he'd given himself up.

Maybe he should take a chance and stay with Damian. The two of them could present a damning picture of the Catholic Church. He would do most of the talking. After all, Damian was still a seventeen-year-old kid. A boy. Trevor was a man. He had matured and grown self-confidant during his twelve years in the reserve. He knew how to talk. He could be a spokesman on behalf of the giants. Maybe that would lead to some kind of employment. The more he thought about it, he decided that it would be stupid of him to leave Damian and Juliet. And now that they were free, he wouldn't need to view Juliet as a romantic partner. He would get a ton of publicity as the spokesman for the giants. He would meet women his age. Women who were more age appropriate.

"Hey, we're moving! Wake up, Juliet!"

Within two minutes they were at the exit.

"We were in that traffic mess for almost an hour," said Trevor.

"Let's get to this guy's house," said Juliet.

Other than the fact that they had to backtrack for three miles, it was clear sailing from this point on. Trevor made a left turn and turned onto an overpass, then it was two miles to Edward Purdell's.

~~~~~~

The monks were having trouble knocking down the wall. The forklifts weren't big enough and were taking too long.

"Ram it into the door," said Brother Terrence. "The foundation will crumble much easier than if we went into the wall itself. Besides, there won't be anything left inside to keep locked up. The giants can come out, then we'll take them straight to the warehouse." He hesitated for a moment and turned to Brother Simon. "Something just dawned on me. When they go into the warehouse it'll be the first time they'll be in a building."

"They've never even seen a building."

The wall finally began to crumble sufficiently to create an exit the giants could get through once the rocks were cleared away.

"Brothers," said Brother Terrence to the fifteen men standing before him. "Let's move the debris to make a walkway for them."

The monks began working feverishly. As they created a large enough space for the giants to walk through Brother Terrence turned to Brother Timothy and said, "Call the news director now."

Within two minutes Brother Timothy had the news director of Channel 5, on the phone. He'd told him about the situation.

"You heard me correctly," said Brother Timothy.

"This isn't some kind of public relations gimmick to sell more jellies and jams, is it?" said Fragoli.

"Far from it. The giants have been kept in the reserve for more than a hundred years and we're setting them free."

"You're for real. I mean, giants, Brother?"

"Giants."

"You been drinking communion wine?"

"I'm telling you the truth."

"How tall are they?"

"Fifteen-to-eighteen feet high."

"Jesus. It's just so hard to believe, but a religious man like yourself wouldn't lie." He paused. "*Would* you?"

"I'll pretend you didn't ask me that. We'll also have the people who've been kept prisoner here by the monks."

"And they'll want to talk to the cameras?"

"I'm certain."

"And this is our exclusive, brother?"

"Yes."

"It would be great if we could get an interview with a giant. Wait a minute. What am I saying? Can they talk?"

"Yes. Perfectly."

He perked up. "You're kidding me."

"Far from it.

"This better not be bullshit, brother. Sorry for my language."

"It's not," said Brother Timothy.

"I'll try to find a reporter who's available," he said. "But I still don't believe you."

"Have them come to the entrance at the eastern side in an hour. That's where we'll be bringing them out."

As Frigoli hung up, he concluded that it was probably some kind of scheme to increase jelly and jam sales or pump up the retreat business. His wife had dragged him to the monastery the year before in an attempt to save their marriage and he wasn't impressed. He decided to send a segment producer and a cameraman in case it was all some kind of scam.

CHAPTER

35

Lieutenant Paul Brantler saw it first out of the corner of his eye. He sat up straight and stared out the chopper's window, adjusting his binoculars. "Sir, on your right. A smiling monk."

Sulpience looked down through his binoculars and saw it too.

"Get on it now!"

The chopper headed towards the exit, but the problem was the trees. Once the truck had exited the highway, they couldn't see it.

"Trees are blocking my view, sir."

"Well, we know which way it's heading."

"Not really. This exit leads to four roads. A cloverleaf. It could be on any one."

"Damnit!" said Sulpience.

~~~~~~

Trevor was concerned as he pulled the truck into Purdell's tree-lined driveway. He noticed that Purdell's home was a restored farmhouse with a barn in the back.

Although there were plenty of trees giving adequate cover from the air, Trevor knew the house wasn't nearly isolated enough. There were neighbors on either side, roughly fifty yards away, but they had clear vision to his property. It was broad daylight. If anyone was looking out the window, they could see Damian when he got out of the truck.

Trevor and Juliet left the box truck and knocked on the front door. Edward answered it. Standing next to him was Teddy Germaine. Before Trevor or Juliet could say a word, Edward spoke.

"Juliet Pine I presume?"

"Yes."

He shook her hand and said, "Edward Purdell. The giant is in the truck?"

"Yes."

"Teddy, did you hear that?"

"I heard it. Boy did I hear it." Teddy was smiling.

"I have to see him."

"We have to get a look right away," said Teddy.

He tried to push by Trevor, who stopped him. "Wait a minute. Who's this guy?"

"Teddy Germaine. He's a believer."

"Pleasure to meet you," said Teddy.

Trevor nodded his head suspiciously.

"Damian needs to get out and stretch," said Juliet.

"He has a name?" asked Edward.

"Yes. They all have names. And numbers. Damian's is six forty-seven. He's the last giant."

"Damian. I'll be damned! Numbers."

"How'd he get a name like Damian?" asked Teddy.

"Wait. Your neighbors will see him when he gets out," said Trevor.

Edward shook his head no. "The people on the left asked me to keep an eye on their house while they're on vacation, so we're good there. The one on the right is an eighty-two-year-old woman who won't be any trouble because she's at her aerobics class right now and then she goes to lunch. We'll be long gone by the time she gets back."

Long gone?

Trevor and Juliet looked at each other.

"All right," said Juliet.

"I've been waiting fifty-six years for this," said Edward.

"For me it's been thirty-two," said Teddy. "I thought it would never happen." Juliet noticed tears in his eyes.

With Teddy behind him, Edward pushed by Trevor and Juliet and walked purposely to the truck. He opened the back doors and took in Damian who was all bunched up. He looked uncomfortable.

"I'm here to save you, son," said Edward.

"If you can find a place where I can stretch me legs, that will be good for starters, mate," said Damian.

"Oh my God, you *do* talk." He turned to Teddy. "He talks, Teddy. And he does sound like a Brit."

"I don't believe it."

"Can we get him out of the truck," said Juliet. "His legs are probably killing him."

"Of course, of course. Come on, my boy. Slide on out of there."

Damian straightened himself out, extended his legs and uneasily slid out. He towered over Edward and Teddy, who just stared at him incredulously.

"Feels good to stretch." He bent his legs over and over again, then walked in a circle.

"Will you look at that," said Edward.

"It's a pleasure to meet you, Damian," said Teddy.

"Yes, it is," said Edward.

"Thank you," said Damian.

Edward stared up and took Damian in. "I took the liberty of removing my vehicles from the barn. You can stand up or stretch or do whatever you want in there. What a magnificent specimen. You're in perfect symmetry to the human body. I'd have thought you would be tall, but hunched over, or even deformed."

Edward turned to Trevor. "How about you? Where do you fit into all of this?"

"I've been a prisoner in the reserve for twelve years."

Edward shook his head back and forth. "Do you believe that, Teddy?"

"I knew it!" said Teddy. "I've been following missing person cases in the area for thirty years. There were too many people who just vanished." He turned to Trevor. "What did you say your name is?"

"Trevor Bruckner."

Teddy scratched his head. "Rings a small bell. There was a story in the paper about how you died in an avalanche. How many others are there?"

"Now, sixteen. Some have died since I got there."

"How did the others get trapped?" asked Teddy.

"Bad luck. They gave me a choice: stay and live or they would kill us. I stayed. They've kept people imprisoned for more than a hundred-and-fifty years."

Teddy seemed interested in the comment. "They have any women prisoners?"

"Yes."

Teddy looked at Edward. "Older women?"

"Yeah. Late sixties and seventies."

"You got somebody there named Katherine?"

"No. Why do you ask?"

He was about to answer when Juliet interrupted him. "Mister Purdell, you said you have a plan?"

"Yes. And call me Edward. A big plan for a big boy. How old are you, son?"

"Seventeen."

Edward looked at Juliet and Trevor. "Which of you is in charge?"

"She is," said Trevor.

"I guess I am," said Juliet.

"We have to move carefully," said Edward. "My guess is that by now the police or the government or someone dangerous is looking for you, specifically for this truck. Most likely in helicopters. Is there anything on the roof of the truck that might give it away?"

"I don't know," said Trevor. "I never thought to look." He turned to Damian. "Could you give the roof a look-see?" Damian moved closer to the truck and looked down. From the look on his face everyone knew something was wrong.

"There's a drawing of a smiling monk," said Damian, his face filled with concern.

"Shit," said Trevor. "We've got to hide the truck too."

"Yes," said Edward. "Of course. Pull it behind the barn and under the oak trees, then I'll tell you my plan."

Trevor got back into the truck. Teddy guided him as he parked it under the trees.

Juliet, Edward and Damian walked to the barn. "We have a plan too," said Juliet.

"Let's hear it," said Edward suspiciously.

"We were going to drive into Manhattan and alert the media. I will speak first, then introduce Damian and let him tell his story."

"That's it?"

"Yes."

"That's not a plan," said Edward. "That's a vague concept. A real plan involves what's going to happen *after* he's introduced to the media."

"Then, what's *your* plan?" asked Jessica, a bit miffed.

Purdell suddenly became serious. "We have to be cautious. We can't let the scientists get their hands on him. We have to protect him."

"How will we do that?" said Trevor.

"I have a friend who'll help us once she gets a look at Damian. Her name is Delilah. Helluva a woman. A real tough nut. She's my ex-wife. She doesn't believe that there are giants in Cassoulet Reserve. Know why? Because I drove her nuts talking about it. That's one of the reasons she divorced me. I wouldn't shut up. But we're friendly. As soon as you called me, I called her to tell her that I was right and she was wrong. When I told her you were bringing Damian to my place she still thought I was conning her. I'm gonna call her and tell her. Hold on." He reached for his cell phone and punched in a number. "He's here, baby doll. Yep. Thirteen, fourteen feet high. He's intelligent. I'm not bullshitting you. It's incredible. Oh, Delilah, the giant talks with a British accent. His name is Damian. Damian, say hello to Delilah."

Damian bent over and got as close to the phone as he could, "Uh, hello, Delilah."

"Purdell, if this is another one of your stupid jokes!" she said.

"It's not. I'm looking at him right now. You gotta come over right now and see him for yourself. And I need a favor. Come here in your horse trailer. I'll need to borrow it and you for a few hours. How soon can you get here? Okay. See you then." He hung up. "She'll be here in twenty minutes."

They got to the barn.

"How can she help us?" said Juliet.

"She breeds horses and has a humongous trailer to move them. Have you ever seen how huge the trucks are that move horses?"

"Not really," said Juliet.

"Trust me. And she's made a ton of money from her third divorce -- I was her first husband -- so she's gonna come in handy for us."

"How?" asked Juliet.

"I'll have Delilah take Damian in her horse transport trailer and bring him to the Lock One Marina downriver where she docks her yacht, which is more than big enough to transport a giant plus all of us." He quickly checked who was there. "Well, maybe not all of us. Three of us. That's all her truck cab will fit."

"Not a problem," said Trevor. "I don't need to go."

"She has her own yacht?" said Juliet.

"I told you she has big bucks."

Juliet looked at Damian and smiled.

"What's a yacht?" Damian asked.

"A big, gigantic boat," she said.

"Then what?" Damian asked. "Where will she take me?"

"We're going to cruise down the Hudson River," said Edward. "No one will be looking for a boat. We'll go to The Statue of Liberty. Symbolic, huh? I love symbolism. I will have contacted the media by then and instructed them to be there with news crews and cameras. We'll make a big splash. I'll tell them that I've been searching for giants all my life, then I'll introduce you to tell them how we came together. You can tell how you escaped from Cassoulet Reserve and then I'll bring you out."

"And you can tell your story, Damian." said Juliet.

"Exactly!" said Purdell. "Damian, my boy, you should start thinking about what you're gonna say."

"I know what I'll say, mate. I'll get straight to the people who put the giants away. The Catholic Church."

"Why do you say that?" Edward asked.

"Because they're responsible for containing the giants all these years."

Edward looked at Teddy. "I knew it! I knew it! How did you find out what the Catholic Church did?"

"Damian and Trevor told me the story, the oral history," said Juliet. "About how the child giants were brought here in the late nineteenth century."

"The child giants were from France, right?" said Edward.

"Yes."

"From Mont Blanc?"

"Yes. A forest near Mont Blanc."

287

Edward looked at Teddy. "Everything that Henri said was true." He turned to Juliet. "Henri is my friend in France. He's a giant hunter too. He learned everything he knows about giants from his great-grandfather who was also a giant hunter. He saw one in 1932. What I've been able to piece together from other folks like me is that sometime in the late nineteenth century the Catholic Church thought they wiped out the giants in Europe, but they didn't get them all. The ones they had were sent to America, to Cassoulet Reserve, although it wasn't called that then."

"Are you saying that they're in Mont Blanc?" asked Damian excitedly.

"No. Not anymore."

Damian looked at Juliet. She felt his frustration at hearing the news.

"Henri heard a rumor that there are more in another location in Europe."

"Where?" asked Juliet.

"He doesn't know for sure, but he's heard stories over the years that it could be Switzerland or Germany."

"Are you *sure* there are no giants in Mont Blanc?" said Damian, heartbroken.

Juliet noticed Damian nervously twirling the ring on his right hand.

"Mister Purdell," she said. "do you know anything about a ring that's been passed down from generation to generation?"

"The ring of Chambéry?"

"I didn't know it had a name," said Juliet.

"How do you know about the ring?" Edward asked with a serious expression.

She pointed at Damian's finger. "Damian is wearing it."

Purdell glanced at Teddy.

"Can I see it, son?" said Edward.

Damian lowered his left hand. Edward studied the ring.

"Where did you get this?"

"My mother gave it to me."

"Where did she get it?"

"From her mother. It was passed down since the child giants were brought over. She told me it came from Mont Blanc. She said it belonged to me and that possessing it was my destiny."

Edward and Teddy looked at each other.

CHAPTER

36

Sulpience had his pilot go as low as he could over all four roads, but they found nothing.

"They must've stopped somewhere in the general area," he said. "They've found an ally. They're undoubtedly going to switch trucks."

"How many people have a spare truck lying around, sir? asked Brantley."

"It won't be a truck. It'll be something else."

"What's bigger than a truck?"

"I don't know."

"There are a lot of farms in this area. Maybe they're going to hide the truck they have in a barn?"

"It'll have to be a pretty big barn. My guess is tall trees that would make it invisible from the sky. They'll probably be waiting for somebody with a bigger vehicle. We have to be on the lookout for anything big enough to hold a giant coming this way. The other question we have to ask ourselves is how long will they hide out? They've got a giant. He needs to eat and sleep. They'll want to keep moving. They stopped for some reason and then they're going to take off, but in a bigger vehicle."

"So, what do we do?"

"Stay in the air and watch for something that's big enough to hold a fifteen-foot giant."

Sulpience's phone rang. He noticed that the return number was from Rome.

"Yes?"

"It's Archbishop Vircuzi. Have you found the giant?"

"Yes and no."

"Explain."

"We found the truck he's in getting off the freeway, but the exits were confusing. Because of the presence of trees, we couldn't narrow down which way the truck went. So, we lost him. But we know the general vicinity he's in."

"If the truck is hidden someplace, you'll never find him. Is that correct?"

Sulpience hesitated. "Not necessarily. It's difficult to hide a box truck. They would need a large building or warehouse to hide it. All they have are trees as cover. I'm certain that with enough time we'll find him."

"We don't have time. How far are your men from Cassoulet Reserve?"

"The choppers I sent are probably forty minutes away by now."

"Listen closely. There's been a change of plans. The monks at St. Alban's have taken control. They're going to release the giants."

"What?"

"I want your men there, but not to eliminate anyone. I want them to help, or at least pretend to help. Instruct your men to tell the media and the survivors that a renegade branch of the Catholic Church was responsible. Tell them that they have come to help and console on behalf of the Pope.

"Archbishop, are you sure?"

"Yes. The damage is done at the reserve. The news of the giants will be out. I want you to concentrate on finding the giant who escaped. If you are correct in your assumption that you will be able to find him, that's good. I will trust that you will do so. Do you have ammunition that can drug a person and knock him out?"

"Yes."

"Enough to render a giant unconscious?"

"Definitely."

"Then drug him."

"Where do I bring him?"

"Is your helicopter big enough to carry him?"

"Yes."

"Fly one hundred miles out into the Atlantic Ocean and dump him."

"May I ask why, Archbishop?"

"Because he's the youngest, the last giant and he started this mess. He must never be seen. And eliminate anyone who is with him."

"Yes, Archbishop."

CHAPTER

37

Brother Timothy saw the lone news truck approach. Two people got out. A cameraman in his fifties wearing a New York Yankees baseball cap who walked with a limp and a female reporter who looked as if she were barely out of high school.

Twenty-three-year-old Liz Cartwright, who had been working at the station for two months on the night shift, got the assignment. Brother Timothy approached her.

"Hello!" he said excitedly. "I didn't think you'd be here so soon. We aren't quite ready for you yet."

"You supposedly have a giant or something big hidden in there," she said brusquely.

"Yes, we do," he said, thinking *another millennial with an attitude.* "Actually, we have eleven."

"Yeah, right." Her tone was sarcastic. He got the feeling that she did not want to be there.

"And there are approximately sixteen normal-sized people who've been imprisoned in there for many years."

She ignored the last piece of information. "I'm here for the giants. My news director wasn't sure the story was legitimate."

"It is."

"You're a monk so you probably wouldn't lie, but are there really giants in that forest? I mean, how can there be giants in there? Where do they come from? And if they're giants, why can't they just knock down the walls?"

"The walls are fortified and much taller than they are," he said.

"How tall are these giants?"

"Some are fifteen feet high."

She made a face. "That's not very tall. Obviously, they're taller than we are, but when I hear the word 'giant' I'm thinking thirty or forty feet high. I mean, they should be gigantic."

"Nope. Tops, maybe twenty feet."

"If you say so," she said, half considering the statement. "Can my cameraman get in there?" She gestured towards the reserve.

"No. The giants will be coming out. As I said, we're not ready to bring them yet."

She shrugged. "How come we're the only news crew here?"

"We didn't want to frighten the giants."

She rolled her eyes. "What would happen if they were frightened?"

"Your guess is as good as mine."

She took in his remark. "Is this for real, father?"

"Brother."

"Sorry. I'm an atheist."

"Yes. This story will put your name on the map."

She arched her right eyebrow. "Or make me a laughing stock and set my career back ten years. Where will they be coming from?" She pointed to the hole in the wall where the brothers were still removing rocks. "There?"

"Yes."

"Kyle," she shouted towards her cameraman. "Let's get set up.

"I'll let you know when they're ready to come out."

"Whatever."

Brother Terrence turned and headed to where the brothers were removing rocks.

As Kyle began unloading his gear, Chief of Police Parterra pulled up and parked his car alongside the news van. He got out and went straight up to Liz.

"What's going on?"

"The station got a call from these monks claiming that they have giants living in the reserve." She rolled her eyes. "Supposedly, they'll be coming out of that big hole over there." She pointed towards where the monks were still removing the rocks.

Chief Parterra again remembered the rumors he'd heard as a boy. "Think there's anything to it?"

"I don't know. The monk I spoke to said that normal sized people will also be coming out."

"What do you mean 'normal' sized?"

"People who've been held captive. I'm personally only interested in seeing the giants."

Captain Parterra stared at the monks who were finishing removing the broken rocks.

He suspected that the rumors he'd heard weren't rumors. He knew he would need backup.

CHAPTER

38

Thirty-five minutes later, Delilah pulled into Edward's driveway in a brand-new, dark blue horse transport trailer smoking a Marlboro light with Springsteen's "Born to Run" blasting from the radio. As soon as Trevor saw the vehicle, he knew that Damian could fit inside comfortably.

She got out of the driver's rig and shouted out Edward's name. "Purdell? Where the hell are you? Purdell?"

Edward stepped out of the barn and shouted, "In the barn, Delilah."

"I want to see this giant," she said firmly, almost demanding.

"Wait right there. We'll bring him to you."

"He better be big or I'll be pissed!"

Edward returned to the barn and within seconds Damian stepped out.

Delilah stared at him with her mouth hanging open. "I don't believe it, but I have to believe it because I'm staring right at him. Jesus Christ!"

"Delilah, we have to get rolling right now," said Edward.

"Why so soon?" she asked.

Damian walked up to Delilah.

"I'm Delilah Branfeld," she shouted up at Damian. "Nice to meet you in person."

"I'm Damian," he said.

"I'll be damned!" She shook her head back and forth. "I'll be damned!"

Juliet, Trevor and Teddy appeared from behind Damian.

Edward turned to Delilah. "I know that someone is looking for this truck and for Damian. We have to keep moving." He looked at Damian. "Sorry to do this to you so soon, but you have to get in this trailer. The only consolation is that it's a little bigger and has more room for you to stretch."

"Okay."

"Open her up," Edward said to Delilah.

She clicked two bars, and the back door opened. Damian crawled inside.

Edward looked at Delilah. "I want to take the boy into Manhattan. We'll need to borrow your yacht?"

"Fine, but I have to make a couple of phone calls to get it ready."

"Start calling."

Delilah took out her cell phone and dialed the first of three numbers.

Edward turned to Juliet. "Your brother said you were on a plane that crashed in the reserve."

"Yes. Damian saved my life."

Edward looked up at Damian. "Good boy. How do you eat? Actually, what I should say is how *much* do you have to eat each day?"

"A lot," said Damian. "I spend each day foraging for food."

"Foraging," said Edward to Teddy. "Who would have thought a giant would use a word like foraging? Incredible!"

"Can I borrow your phone?" asked Juliet. She wanted to call her brother back.

"Sure, honey," said Edward. He handed her his iPhone.

Juliet put in her brother's number. "Greg? I'm okay. We're all okay."

"Where are you?"

"Mister Purdell's."

"Thank God."

"Did you call CNN?"

"Yes. They hung up on me."

"What? Why?"

"I told them everything you told me to say and, well, I think they thought I was crazy."

Juliet felt uneasy. "That's okay. I'll do it."

"I don't know, Juliet. The person I talked to was pretty dismissive of me. It was like she thought I was a prank caller. Then I called MSNBC and I even tried FOX. They all said the same thing. It was like they knew I was calling."

"Don't worry about it, Greg. I'll handle it."

"When are you coming back?"

"Probably tomorrow. I want to make sure that Damian is safe."

"Can't you leave him with that Purdell guy? Can't he do it?"

"No. I'm Damian's friend. I promised him I'd stay with him until he was safe."

"Juliet... "

"I'm okay. Really. You can relax. I have to go. I love you, Greggy."

"I love you too, Juliet." In the excitement of talking to his sister, he forgot to tell her that he had called Chief Parterra.

Juliet hung up. She was concerned that CNN and the other networks blew off her brother.

"Mister Purdell?" she said.

"Edward. Call me Edward."

"My brother called CNN, MSNBC and FOX to tell them we had a giant that's been held prisoner. They weren't interested. Wouldn't you be interested in a story like that if you were a CNN news editor?"

Edward looked tense. "That means somebody got to them. I wish you hadn't told him to call. These things have to be handled a certain way."

"Sorry."

"Don't worry about it, Juliet. See, reporters are a suspicious lot. Most of them are know-it-alls. Even when they're handed a story, they're filled with doubt. So, what we have to do is show them the story."

"I don't understand."

"To make big news you have to think big. That's why we're going to The Statue of Liberty. That's when all the networks will have their cameras buzzing."

CHAPTER

39

"I only have room for two people," said Delilah. She turned to Edward. "I know you're going. So, of these three who's coming along? Hi Teddy."

"Hi Delilah. We really appreciate you doing this."

"My pleasure. So, who's the third?"

"I am," said Juliet. She turned to Trevor. "Are you sure?"

"Yes," said Trevor. "I wish you both good luck."

Juliet walked up to Trevor and hugged him. "Thanks for all your help. Do you want to say goodbye to Damian?"

Trevor nodded his head and moved close to the trailer. Damian's head was facing him.

"This is it, friend," he said.

"Yeah. You gonna be alright, mate?"

"I'll be fine. You're the one I'm worried about." He extended his hand. Damian touched it with his right fingertip. Have a good life, Damian."

"You too."

Trevor turned and stepped away as Delilah locked Damian inside.

"Are we ready?" said Edward, then he climbed into the front.

"Let's boogie!" said Delilah. "Everybody buckled in?"

Juliet and Edward said yes.

"Let's get this giant to the Big Apple!" said Delilah, then she pulled out of the yard.

Trevor watched as the horse trailer drove out of sight, then he walked to where Teddy was standing. Teddy looked at the semi parked under the trees. "What's gonna happen with that truck?"

"I'm thinking of taking it," said Trevor.

"To where?"

"Marbery. My brother lives there. At least I think he does."

"Give him a call. You can use my phone?" Teddy extended his iPhone to Trevor who stared at it.

"Thanks, but I don't remember his number."

"I wouldn't drive in the truck if I were you. You'd be an open target. Tell you what, Marbery's not that far from here. I don't mind driving you."

"Really?"

"Yeah. I can bring you up to speed on what's been happening in the world since you've been away."

"Sounds good."

"You ready? I'm almost tempted to stop at my place to check my files. I know I heard your name before."

"Do you have some clothes that I could borrow, Teddy?"

"Sure do. I'll set you up."

"Thanks."

They walked to Teddy's car, got in and drove off.

"How did you get interested in giants?" asked Trevor.

"It wasn't giants at first. I was interested in the missing people."

"Why?"

"My wife disappeared. I've been convinced all these years that somehow, she got swallowed up in the reserve. See, we both loved hiking. There were trails on and around Hammerhead Mountain, which were our favorite places to trek. Most times we would go out together, but because we had what you might call a volatile relationship, I was a screamer and she was a thrower, when we needed to get away from each other, we went separately. One day, after a particularly nasty argument, I stormed out of the house. When I got back that night, my wife wasn't there. I noticed that her hiking boots were gone so I assumed she went for a hike at Hammerhead Mountain to cool off. When she didn't return that night or the next day, I reported her missing to the police. They searched the hiking paths, but found no trace of her. That's when I became convinced that the reserve and the giants had taken her."

"Sorry, man," said Trevor.

"From that day forward, I tried to gain access to the reserve. I covered not only the hiking paths, but the woods surrounding them. I tried climbing the steep, jagged mountain hoping to find some kind of entrance into Cassoulet Reserve, but I couldn't. I failed again and again. Finally, I came to the realization that I'd never find or see her again. I gave up. My wife was never heard from again."

"How long ago did she disappear?"

"Thirty-six years. I think about her every day."

"If she was in the reserve, I would have known her. What's her name?"

"Katherine."

Trevor shrugged his shoulders. "I don't know anyone by that name. She wasn't there, at least for the last twelve years. Anything before that I don't know. Sorry."

"You're saying she could have passed away."

"Yeah."

Teddy mulled over the statement. "Did a lot of the people trapped in there die?"

"I don't really know about the people who came before me, but I'd say yes. We had a little cemetery. I don't recall ever seeing a grave marker with the name Katherine on it."

"Ah," said Teddy glumly.

They drove in silence.

CHAPTER

40

As Martin waited for everyone to arrive, he tried to figure out what Damian's plan was. Or was it the girl's plan? Damian had no contacts outside the reserve. He assumed it could not be the same for Trevor. He was young enough to have some friends and family. He decided that it had to be the girl. She would probably call someone. He suspected the first place they would be heading was to a telephone. He had learned about telephones from one of the mountain climbers under his care who had worked for Verizon. He learned much of what the outside world was like from various abnormals.

Something dawned on him. He knew that if Damian succeeded in exposing the monks, it would be big news. Cassoulet Reserve would be swarming with people. And he knew that being out beyond the reserve would mean being a different kind of prisoner.

If Damian, Trevor and the girl were stopped or captured before they could make a call and tell what's been going on, it would mean that all three would be killed, he was certain of it.

A fatalistic idea crossed his mind. He knew that even if he were set free, there would be no freedom. He and the other giants would be contained somewhere. He would be a prisoner of his own freedom.

He suspected that he would have to make a choice. Live and be put in a new prison or die. He decided that he would rather die, but he was determined to take the Abbot and as many monks as he could with him.

At that moment, Pete made his way to where Martin told him to go. It was the first time he'd seen Martin in almost two years.

"What's this all about?" asked Pete. He noticed a monk sitting on the ground behind Martin, although he didn't know it was Abbot Gassner.

"They're letting us go."

"The monks?" Pete was stunned. "Why?"

"There are men coming here to kill us. I talked to a monk who says that setting us free is the only way to save us."

Pete smirked. "I don't believe it. He's setting us up."

"No. He's telling the truth, Pete. It's really happening."

"I'm not leaving."

"It's our one chance to get out."

D. B Gilles

"And do what? And live where? In another government sponsored prison?"

"I told him I wanted him to come in here with us."

"For what?"

"I wanted him to see us and the abnormals and how we live."

"He won't care and he won't come."

"He's here." Martin looked down over Pete's shoulder and saw Abbot Gassner lying on the ground.

"I'd like to kill him," said Pete as he glared at Gassner.

"I was thinking the same thing, but I decided it would be too easy. I think we should let him live."

"Live? After what he's done to us?"

"I didn't finish. I think we should let him live... in here... with us."

"Make him our prisoner?" said Pete.

"Yeah. Let him understand what it's like."

"What about leaving? Aren't you going to go?"

"And do what?" said Martin.

"My feelings exactly."

"But the abnormals will all go. They'll tell the truth. Everyone will know we're here."

"It'll be suicide if we leave. Sooner or later someone will capture us and..."

"I know. If we stay, who will be in charge?"

"Do you want to?"

"No. I'm too old. Besides, I don't have much time left."

Martin acknowledged the comment. "Then I'll do it."

"We need a truce."

"Yes." Martin extended his right hand. Pete shook it.

"What I think we should do, or you can do it, is say something to the people out there."

"Like what?"

"I don't know. Just something."

"Why don't you? We'll all go out and you can say whatever you want."

"No. We should stay inside. Let them come in."

"Okay. When they're all here, tell them we're not going anywhere and that you'll be making a speech."

Martin nodded yes and looked down at Gassner.

"Did you hear any of what we were talking about?"

"No. You were too far away."

"Do you like it here?"

"Not particularly."

"Too bad."

"What do you mean?"

"Abbot Gassner, meet Pete. Pete, Abbot Gassner."

"Hand him to me, Martin," said Pete.

D. B Gilles

"Sure thing." Martin reached down, scooped up Abbot Gassner roughly and handed him to Pete who kept him in his right hand."

"Where are you taking me?" said the abbot.

"To your new home," said Pete who nodded to Martin.

Martin looked up. "Wait. Here come the others."

The remaining giants made their way to the entrance, as did the regular-sized people who could walk. Those who couldn't were picked up and carried by a few of the giants. A rag-tag collection of senior citizens stood before Martin.

"Something we never thought would happen has happened," Martin declared. "The monks are setting us free."

Instead of a wild cheer there was only silence. After so many years in captivity the capacity for joy was gone. Then Margo spoke.

"Is this for real or just bullshit?" she asked.

"It's real."

"Why? Why now?"

"Damian has escaped." The remark prompted some mumbling from the crowd. "So did Trevor and the girl who survived the plane crash."

"Her name is Juliet," said Gretchen.

"She was gonna be our cook," said Victor.

Gretchen smiled.

"The man in charge of the monastery, Abbot Gassner, has told us we are free. Pete, show him off."

314

Pete showed Gassner off as if he were a pet turtle. The giants all stared at him in silence. Pete placed him back on the ground. The giants and the others moved closer, surrounding him in a circle.

They all stared at him.

"I've been here almost forty years," said Margo.

"A man in his late seventies said, "I've been here for forty-two years. I had a wife, children, parents and family you bastard."

One by one, each regular-sized person laid into him.

"I'm sorry," said Gassner. "I did it to protect the Catholic Church."

"I did nothing wrong," said Gretchen. "None of us did. I was a Catholic. I was a lector at my church."

"I don't know what to say," said Gassner in a whisper.

"I have nothing, no one," said the old man.

"What will we do for money?"

"How will we survive?"

"I'm an old man, how can I work?"

"When I was young, I was beautiful, now I'm an old hag."

"How do we get the hell out of here?" said Margo.

Martin raised his hand towards the entrance door and pointed.

The regular-sized people made their way to the door. A brother was waiting for them. One by one they stepped out of the reserve and into freedom.

"Now what?" said Gretchen.

"Where's my car?" said a bald, skinny old man.

"You've been here for more than thirty years," said Gretchen. "I doubt they'll have your car."

"I liked that car," he replied. "Toyota Corolla."

Brother Terrence spoke. "I know this is probably overwhelming for you... "

"I want to go home," shouted a man.

"Me too!" said another.

"I don't know if my family will even be around, but I want to try to contact them," said a woman.

Gretchen was the first one out. Waiting outside of the gate were the monks who'd cleared the path. They stared at her and she stared at them.

Then, one by one all the regular-sized people made their way out.

"Should I get these people on a B roll, Liz?" the cameraman asked.

"Yes, but where are the giants? If these people have been captives that'll be a decent story, but the real story is the giants."

Then, she saw Martin as he stepped outside.

"Oh my God!" She looked up and stared with her mouth hanging open at Martin. "Get him! Get this fucking giant!"

The cameraman, equally shocked, began filming.

Martin stepped through the entrance the monks made, over the rocks. He stared out over everything, taking it all in. He saw buildings, cars, trucks, cement

316

roads and people wearing clothes that he'd never seen staring at him. He was both awestruck and terrified.

Chief Parterra couldn't take his eyes off of Martin.

Brother Terrence approached Liz Cartwright. "It was my idea to call your boss and have him send you here."

"Incredible," she said. "Just incredible. Is he going to say anything? I mean, can he talk?"

"Oh yes." Terrence turned and looked up at Martin. "If you want to say anything, now is the time." He pointed at the camera. "Just talk in this direction."

Martin looked down at the camera, not quite sure what it was, in a daze.

"I'll go first," said Terrence. He looked into the camera.

"I am Brother Terrence of the St. Alban's Monastery and Retreat House. For more than a hundred years we have been holding captive the last remaining giants in the world."

Several workers noticed Martin. Six of them pulled out their iPhones and began filming as Terrence spoke.

"Today we are setting them free. One of them, his name is Martin, will speak on the others behalf." He gestured to Martin.

Martin took several moments to get used to being outside. He was transfixed by the monastery, the cars and trucks in the distance. He saw Abbot Gassner's bicycle and stone roads. He was overwhelmed as he took it all in. Then he spoke.

"The Catholic Church has held us prisoner in this place and our ancestors in other places around the world for thousands of years."

As he spoke, Liz turned to Brother Terrence. "What are you going to do with them?"

"For now, I don't know."

"Can I ask him some questions?"

"I think for now you should just get him on film. I want the world to know about the giants of Hammerhead Mountain, but you can ask the normal-sized people anything you want."

"Okay. This is going to win me a Pulitzer fucking Prize."

Chief Parterra listened too. What ran through his mind was different than what Liz McCormick was thinking. He knew that once the news feed got out the place would be swarming with media. He had five men on his police force on their way. He knew they wouldn't be able to handle a crowd, so he decided to put a call into the New York State Troopers.

He was just about ready to dial when he saw four helicopters approaching.

CHAPTER

41

Trevor was about to nod off. Even though Teddy was the kind of person who liked to pass the time talking, he let him rest. He knew Trevor was exhausted and that he faced an uncertain future. He turned the radio on softly to listen to a talk show, but what he heard shook him up so much he almost lost control of his vehicle.

"In upstate New York, in a government protected nature reserve called Cassoulet, next to the popular hiking routes of Hammerhead Mountain, it was revealed today that eleven giants lived there. That's right. Giants. As in Jack and the Beanstalk. The giants are the last survivors of a race of giants that have been kept prisoner in the reserve since the late nineteenth century. One of them, who goes by the name of Martin, spoke on camera."

Teddy shook Trevor awake.

"Do you know a giant named Martin?" asked Teddy.

"Yeah," said Trevor trying to wake up. "Why?"

"Listen. He's talking."

Trevor shook the sleep out of his eyes and leaned in towards the radio.

"I can talk and I can think and I can use reason," Martin continued. "Today we were given the chance to be free, but we decline the offer. Most of us are staying inside Cassoulet Reserve because it has been our home and it's all we know. We're afraid that if we do leave, we'll be taken prisoner and turned over to your scientists to figure us out. One of us has decided to leave and I wish him well. His name is Damian. He wants to go to a place across the ocean called Mont Blanc where there are other giants. The Catholic Church is responsible for putting our ancestors here, and there, and keeping us prisoner. There are sixteen abnormals who have been held against their will for many years. Many of them have died over the years. We hold the Catholic Church responsible for them as well. They have already left the reserve, hopefully to be reunited with their families. Look at me. I am a giant. I am twenty-six years old, which is like fifty-six in human years. I am a prisoner. My captors are the Catholic Church. Who will hold them responsible? If they mean it that we are being set free, then let us be. We don't want it."

Martin then stepped back inside the reserve.

The newscaster came back on and said, "Harsh accusations. More to come later."

Trevor and Teddy looked at each other.

"I better call, Edward," said Teddy. He grabbed his iPhone and hit Edward's number.

"Hello?"

"Did you hear?"

"Hear what?"

"The giants have been released."

"What?"

"It's on the news," said Teddy. "Turn on a radio or check your cell phone or an iPad. A giant came out of the reserve and spoke. He hit the Catholic Church hard. Blamed it all on them. There are eleven giants left. He said they don't want to be free, then he went back into the reserve."

Edward was dumbstruck and furious. He stared straight ahead through the dashboard window trying to figure out what to do.

"I'll keep you posted," said Teddy, then hung up. He turned to Trevor. "Are you up for going back to Cassoulet Reserve?"

Trevor was stunned by the question. "Why would I want to go back there?"

"To help the survivors that are coming out," said Teddy. "You could be their spokesman. You could tell their side of the story."

Trevor hesitated, then said, "All right."

Trevor was uneasy. "Who will I be talking to?"

"The media," said Teddy.

"Won't they be gone by the time we get there?"

"Are you kidding me? This is the biggest story in the world."

Teddy gunned the accelerator. "We'll be there in twenty minutes.

~~~~~~

"What's going on, Edward?" said Juliet.

"The monks have let everyone in the reserve go. One giant came out and spoke."

"That's good," said Juliet. "Now people will know that giants exist."

"No. Now we can't do what I wanted to do. They stole my thunder. I wanted to be the one who presented Damian to the world. He's young. Handsome. Who wants to listen to an old giant talk? Damian had to be the one."

"Then, how can we steal it back?" said Delilah.

"What?"

"Your thunder. Good Lord, Purdell, we've got a giant in the back of this rig. Surely we can do something with him. Why not stick to the original plan? Statue of Liberty. That sounded pretty impressive to me."

"By the time we got there the news will be all over the world. Somebody recorded the giant talking, so there are probably news crews, sending everything the giant said out to the world. And who knows how many people will get it or have already gotten it on their iPhones?"

"In that case, we have to do something bigger," said Juliet.

Edward looked at her. "Like what?"

"He wanted to go to France, where he thinks there are more giants."

"I told you, there are no giants in France," said Edward. "They're somewhere else. And how would we even get there?"

Delilah interjected. "You wanted The Statue of Liberty. Let's take him to an even better symbol."

Edward was confused. "Where?"

"Paris. The Eiffel Tower. The Seine starts in The Atlantic Ocean. We can pull right up to it."

"Maybe we should find out what Damian wants to do," said Juliet.

"You're right." He turned around and looked at Damian.

"Where do you want to go, son?"

"If Mont Blanc doesn't have giants anymore, I don't know."

"I just got an idea," said Delilah. "Screw the yacht. Let's take a plane."

"How will we get a plane?" said Juliet.

"Not a problem. I can borrow my friend's private jet. It's at Teterboro Airport."

"Who's gonna fly it?" said Juliet.

"Me," said Juliet.

Edward said, "She's a handy woman."

"Since we're going to Teterboro, we'll forget about the yacht. We'll just go straight to the airport."

"Is Damian safe now?" said Juliet.

"No. He's in more danger than ever."

"From who?" asked Juliet.

"Who do you think? The Catholic Church. They'll want him out of the picture."

"But why? The giants and everyone will be on the news. What do they want from Damien?"

"He's the youngest giant. The last one. He has to be watched over."

"I need to call my friend who owns the jet."

"And I need to call my giant hunter friend who lives in Mont Blanc."

Juliet turned around and looked at Damian.

"You're going to Paris," she said happily. "You're going to Paris!"

CHAPTER

42

"**I**'ve been meaning to ask you, how did you manage to escape from Cassoulet Reserve?" asked Teddy. "I mean, where was the exact point? Reason I ask is because I scouted Hammerhead Mountain a hundred times looking for a way in and I found nothing."

"Makes sense. It was a fissure in the rocks. A fluke. Natural erosion. Damian found it. When was the last time you looked?"

"It's been years. Probably ten years. After Katherine first disappeared, I went up to Hammerhead Mountain every weekend. Did it for years. Then it became once every two weeks, then once a month, then four times a year until I pretty much gave up looking for someplace to get inside the reserve. God, I miss Katherine."

"I know how hard it must have been, being on the other end," said Trevor. After a few seconds, he had a thought. "Did your wife have a nickname or some other name people called her?"

"Yeah. Margo. I hated that. I always called her Katherine, which she couldn't stand."

"Margo?" Trevor smiled excitedly. "Teddy, Margo is one of the people I take care of."

"You're kidding me."

"If it's the same person, your wife is alive! How old is she?"

"My age. Sixty-eight."

"What's her personality like?"

"Pretty cantankerous. She has a real temper. Kind of a bitch, but she had a good heart and I loved her. I never knew how she'd be from day to day. Not that I was all that easy to live with."

"Always complaining and whining about things?" said Trevor.

"That's my girl."

"Then it's definitely her."

"Now we have an even better reason to get to Cassoulet Reserve."

"How much longer till we get there?"

"Ten minutes if the traffic's good."

Teddy floored the accelerator.

CHAPTER

43

Archbishop Vircuzi stared at his phone, perspiring. It looked as if he might come out of this unscathed. He was fearful about the call he had to make to the pope. He had always been secretly proud of the fact that he had his direct number and he always got right through.

But this? The church's darkest secret now exposed? He didn't know what to expect. He decided to get it over with. He was certain that he would be banished from his beloved Rome and sent to a Godforsaken parish somewhere.

He was about to dial the number when his phone rang. He recognized the number as coming from the Vatican's area code. He took a deep breath and answered.

"Archbishop Vircuzi."

"Good afternoon. This is Cardinal Giraldi, prefect to the pope."

Vircuzi recognized the name immediately as the pope's closest aide. "Yes. I know who you are, your Excellency."

As prefect to the pope his job was to organize the pontiff's daily round of audiences and meetings. That was the official definition of his duties, but within the Vatican it was common knowledge that job meant he always had the pope's ear and more often than not, his counsel.

"I know why you're calling, your Excellency," continued Vircuzi. "I'm sorry for the events of the last twenty-four hours. There was such short notice, I…"

"The damage is done. The news has been broadcast throughout the world. The pope has seen it. He will be issuing a statement denying any knowledge."

"Of course. I will take full responsibility."

"That won't be necessary. We're putting the blame on an offshoot of Opus Dei." Opus Dei is a Roman Catholic organization of laymen and priests founded in Spain in 1928 with the aim of re-establishing Christian ideals in society. "Let them say what they want. As for the pope, he welcomes the giants into the church. We will put them up in a more humane place. Most are old. They will die soon and the world will forget."

"What about the young one? Number six-forty-seven? He's been captured. I can do to him whatever the pope wishes."

"About that. The giant who spoke said that six-forty-seven said he wants to go to a place where there are other giants, yes?"

"Yes. Mont Blanc. But the giants there are long gone."

"There is another place where he should go."

Vircuzi was confused. "Another place?"

"Yes. Only a handful know, less than a handful. The Pontiff, obviously, myself and Cardinal Pontio."

Vircuzi knew Cardinal Pontio. He was a hardliner from the twentieth century who had trained under Cardinal Ratzinger, known as God's Rottweiler, and later named Pope Benedict XVI.

Vircuzi wanted to ask why he hadn't been informed of this other place where giants were, but decided not to. He would wait to be told.

"It is in Germany. The Black Forest Nature Reserve."

"I've never heard of it."

"It's protected land in the mountains about sixty miles from Ramstein Air Base. It serves as headquarters for the United States Air Forces in Europe, Air Forces Africa and also for NATO Allied Air Command. We maintain it. There are giants there. The pope wants six-forty-seven taken there. Let him live out his life with his people."

"Yes, Archbishop, but..."

"Do you have a problem with the pope's wishes?"

"I've been in charge of the American giants for nearly thirty-six years. I was told that the ones in New

York State were the last. I'm wondering why this new place wasn't revealed to me."

"When the Templers removed the child giants at the end of the nineteenth century, they left their parents at Mont Blanc. Their thinking was that the remaining giants would die. The mission was thought to be completed. Then a new batch of giants were found several years later. The powers that be felt that the giants living in the States were settled and to bring in a large group of new child giants would be disruptive, so they were taken to The Black Forest and promptly forgotten about. Why you weren't informed of them, I don't know, but you're in the loop now. Carry it out as quickly as possible. It's an easy flight. Have the Templar you're working with land at Ramstein Air Base. A helicopter will be waiting to take six-forty-seven to his final destination. Here are the directions. Do you have a pen?"

"Yes."

CHAPTER

44

When Teddy and Trevor pulled up to the gate at the monastery, there were several other news crews and four helicopters that had landed, but since Martin had returned to the reserve, there wasn't much happening.

Teddy noticed a group of old women and men standing together and grumbling. The monks had gotten them water and food. Several armed and dangerous-looking solders were talking to them.

"I want to get closer," said Teddy. "I came back to look for Katherine." He got out of his car.

"Wait for me," said Trevor. "I'll go with you. I've got to find out what's been happening."

With Teddy walking ahead of him, Trevor fell behind because of his crippled foot. As Teddy approached the crowd of elderly survivors he stopped and stared at all the women. He was stunned because they were all dressed alike in gray or black dresses and they looked alike: old, beaten down and broken. His last image of Katherine was of a beautiful, lusty thirty-two-year-old woman. The women he was staring at all looked as if they could be in their seventies or eighties.

He was overwhelmed.

Trevor stepped up to Teddy. "Do you see her?"

"I see old women."

"Teddy, she *is* old. So are *you*." He turned his attention to the crowd. "There she is."

"Where?"

"C'mon, I'll take you to her." He took Teddy by the arm and walked him towards a white-haired woman who looked like an older version of his wife. He strained his eyes.

"Is that her?" he asked. "Is that Katherine?

He couldn't tell. He needed to get a closer look.

Teddy approached the crowd of regular-sized people who were also staring as if in a daze. He zoned in on the woman Trevor said was his wife. He walked up to her. He was shaking. He looked at her face closely. She noticed him ogling her.

"What the hell are *you* looking at?" she snarled.

"Katherine," he said sheepishly, still not certain it was she.

Margo stared at him.

"Margo?" said Trevor. "This is Teddy. Your husband."

She looked back at him, her eyes two slits as she strained to see him. Then her face drained of all color.

"Teddy?"

"Yes."

"Oh Teddy!" she said. "Is that really you?"

He moved up to her and held her in his arms. They both started crying.

"I figured you'd have found somebody else," she said.

"I marry for life," said Teddy.

Margo noticed Trevor. "What are you doing here? I heard that you left with Damian and the young girl."

"I came back when I heard they let the giants out," said Trevor. "Teddy talked me into it."

"Good boy," she said as she tapped Teddy affectionately on the top of his head. She was smiling. It was the first time Trevor had ever seen her smile.

The reporter was taking it all in, trying to gather her thoughts. "Are you getting this, Kyle?" she shouted.

"Yes. Yes, I am. I don't believe it."

"Look. That guy is hugging one of the survivors. Let's go talk to them."

She ran over to them. "Hi, Liz McCormick from PBS. What is it like to be reunited with your loved one after all these years?"

"How the hell do you think it feels?" Margo snarled. "Is that camera on?"

"Yes. Say anything you want."

Margo stared into the lens. "I am gonna sue the Catholic Church for keeping me prisoner in this Godforsaken place for the last thirty-six years. If there are any lawyers out there interested in representing me, I'll be waiting for your call. My name is Margo Germaine. I'm in the book."

"Nobody uses telephone books anymore, honey," said Teddy. He turned to the camera and said, "Just Google Teddy Germaine and she'll get the message."

"You looking for somebody to interview?" asked Trevor.

"Who are you? I didn't see you come out with them?"

"I didn't. I got out earlier today. I escaped with another giant, but I came back to tell our story."

~~~~~~

It was the smart phones belonging to the workers in the plant that spread the word, even more so than Liz Cartwright's news broadcast, which was picked up by news agencies worldwide. The video of Martin talking went viral. They got Trevor talking on behalf of the normal-sized survivors. Albert Sulpience's men tried to tell everyone that a renegade branch of the Catholic Church was responsible and that they were there to help, but no one believed them.

How could they?

The Pope gave a press conference in which he invited the giants to leave Cassoulet Reserve, but they all declined. The pontiff stuck with the story blaming Opus Dei for being responsible for keeping the giants prisoner.

Although the giants chose not to leave, Martin did allow medical personnel to come inside to treat the giants who needed attention.

CHAPTER

45

Delilah pulled off at the next exit and on the overpass swung the vehicle around to get back on the freeway. She knew that Damian was heavy, but she had miscalculated how much he actually weighed. In her excitement she turned too fast and lost control. The horse trailer turned completely over and the suddenness of the crash opened the locked back door, throwing Damian half in and half out of the rig.

One of the choppers heading south spotted it first. He radioed to Sulpience who was still circling in another one.

"Sir, I got him."

"Where?"

"On exit forty-eight going south. He's in a horse trailer. There's been an accident. I can see his legs hanging out. What should I do?"

"Get him and hold him and whoever he's with until I get there. If he tries to run do not shoot. Use the drug canisters and knock him out."

"Yes sir."

Edward and Delilah were both unconscious. Juliet was awake, but uninjured.

"Damian!?" she screamed. She shoved the door on the passenger side open and climbed out.

"Damian!" she screamed as she ran to the back of the horse trailer. She saw his legs dangling out.

"Are you all right?" she said as she looked inside.

"Yes, but something's wrong with my leg. I think it might be broken."

"Oh no," said Juliet. "I don't know what to do. Edward and Delilah are both unconscious, the trailer is turned over, you can't walk. I... "

She was interrupted by the sounds of a helicopter coming in for a landing.

"Damian, can you run?"

"I don't think so."

"Then, this is it." She turned and watched as the chopper came to a stop. Four soldiers carrying weapons jumped out and approached her and Damian.

"Get on the ground," one of them screamed.

"He can't," said Juliet. "I think his leg is broken. Please don't hurt him."

"Get on the ground and put your hands behind your back."

"He speaks English, perfect English. He can understand everything you say."

"Get on the ground!" the same solder screamed.

"If you'll tell him what you want him to do, he will do it," said Juliet. "He's not violent. He's gentle."

The soldier who was screaming at her, looking at another soldier and whispered something to him. Then he turned back to Juliet.

"Tell him to get out of the rig now."

"There's no need for her to tell me," said Damian. "I heard you."

All eight soldiers were stunned that he could speak. Each one pointed his gun at him.

Slowly, Damian slid out of the horse trailer. With great difficulty he lay down on the ground. The soldiers didn't know what to do or even say. Then, Sulpience's chopper arrived. He got out and observed the giant prone before him on the ground.

"He speaks English, sir," said one of the soldiers. "He'll understand anything you say."

"Block off the highway," said Sulpience. "We don't want anyone seeing him. Put your chopper in the road about a hundred yards back. That should do it."

"Please don't hurt him," said Juliet.

"That is not my intention." He moved closer to Damian. "Can you move?"

"A little. I think my leg is broken."

Hearing him speak unsettled Sulpience for several seconds. "Can you walk to my helicopter?"

"I think so."

"Then do it."

Pointing to the other chopper, he looked at Juliet said, "You get into that one."

"Where are you taking him?" said Juliet.

"To a safe place."

"Can I come with him?"

"No."

Damian stopped walking. "I want her to come with me. Let her and I'll get on peacefully. If not, there will be trouble."

Sulpience considered the statement. "Okay. Get in."

Juliet ran to Damian and together they got into Sulpience's chopper. They stared at each other in silence, then, without warning Sulpience himself fired three drug pellets into Damian, knocking him out completely. Juliet was so stunned, she couldn't even scream, then she felt one pellet hit her. She too fell unconscious.

Sulpience immediately called Archbishop Vircuzi in Sienna.

"I have the giant," he said. "Are your orders still to drop him into the Atlantic Ocean?"

"No," said Vircuzi. "The monks were true to their word. They have released a giant and he has spoken to the public. The news has spread all over the world. The church has already dealt with it. I've received new orders. You're taking six-forty-seven to a different place. You'll need a different aircraft, something that will withstand a nine-hour flight."

"Where am I taking him?"

"First to Ramstein Air Base in Germany, then to a nature reserve hidden in the Italian Alps."

CHAPTER

46

The flight to Ramstein Air Base actually too ten-and-a-half hours. Sulpience was given a C-5M Super Galaxy military plane, the biggest military transport aircraft used by the United States.

Damian was conscience, but secured in chains. He could not break free. He and Juliet were kept separated throughout the flight.

Sulpience was curious as to how Juliet fit into the escape plan. He wanted to talk about it, but she was too petrified to contribute much to the conversation.

"The plane I was in crashed," she said. "I was the only survivor. Damian saved me. We became friends. That's it."

"Friends? In five days?"

"Yes," she said defiantly.

"There has to be more."

"He said he found a way out and asked me to help. I said okay because I wanted to get out. Where are you taking us?"

"How?" said Sulpience.

"How what?"

"How did he want you to help?"

"He wanted me to drive a truck."

"How did he know what a truck is? He's never seen a truck in his life."

"I didn't ask."

"You drove a truck?"

"No. Trevor did."

"Who's Trevor?"

"He escaped with us."

"Where is he now?"

"I don't know. He left."

"He left. Okay, what was your plan?"

"To get away."

"Where were you going to go?"

"The Statue of Liberty, but that was before the monks let the giants out. Where are we going?"

"To another reserve."

"Is it in France?"

Sulpience said nothing.

"Would you please tell me where?"

"You'll find out soon enough."

"Is it Mont Blanc? That's where Damian always wanted to go."

Sulpience said nothing.

"Are you going to kill him?" asked Juliet.

"Six forty-seven?"

"His name is Damien."

"No."

"Are you going to kill me?"

"Don't you think that if I were going to kill you, I would have done it by now?"

They were both silent for several seconds, then Sulpience spoke. "By the way, you can tell your 'friend' that his leg wasn't broken. I had a doctor look at it. He pulled a hamstring. He'll be fine."

"Thank you."

"As far as where we're taking you, let's just say that he's going to get what he wanted. I'll leave it at that."

What does he mean?

"Would you please tell me something about where you're taking us?" Juliet begged.

Sulpience stared at her for several seconds, then said, "You're going to a nature reserve in Germany."

"Thank you," said Juliet.

"And it's escape proof," Sulpience added ominously.

A helicopter was waiting for them on the runway. Damian and Juliet were led into the chopper. The flight to the nature reserve in Italy took sixty-five minutes. The helicopter landed in a tiny area surrounded by trees. It resembled the Cassoulet Reserve. The door opened and they were told to get out.

Damian went first, then Juliet stepped out. Before Sulpience closed the door, he said, "You're in a secret piece of land owned and maintained by The Vatican. Like where you were in The States, it is a no-flyover-zone. They call it the white forest. Giants have been here for a hundred-and-thirty years. You both can thank the Pope for this. My original orders were to kill you."

Juliet and Damian looked at each other. "There are giants here," said Juliet barely containing her excitement.

"One more thing," said Sulpience. "Six-forty-seven? You won't be so unique around here."

He smirked and closed the door. Within seconds, the helicopter was flying away.

"What did he mean by that?" asked Damian, sounding concerned.

"I don't know. I guess we'll find out."

Damian looked around, taking the new place in. "All these trees. Looks exactly like where we came from."

"I wonder where the giants are," said Juliet.

"Let me try to find out," said Damian, then he raised his hands to his mouth, cupped them and made several strange sounds that echoed around them like what Martin did in Cassoulet Reserve.

"What's that?" said Juliet, confused.

"An announcement that we're here. Giant talk."

"What did you say?" said Juliet.

"I said we just got here and that we'll be walking towards the mountain, over there." He pointed towards the closest mountain top.

"Why to the mountain?"

"Caves. We have to look for a cave for shelter." He turned to his left and looked upwards. "I told them we're going to the closest one." He bent over and extended his hand. Without question, Juliet stepped into it and Damian pulled her up and put her on his right shoulder. "Ready?"

"Yes. You better go slowly."

"I have no reason to run," said Damian. "There are no territories here."

"What the guy who brought us here said, about giants being here for a hundred plus years, that's good, right, Damian?"

"I think so. I hope so."

"I wonder if they'll speak English," said Juliet.

"Why wouldn't they?"

"Every country in the world speaks their own language. He said we're in Italy so they should speak Italian, but most countries have English as a second language. Most kids grow up learning to speak English because everybody in the world wants to come to America."

"Who would have taught the giants to speak English?"

Juliet pondered the question. "I don't know."

"Unless an abnormal-sized person were here, they wouldn't speak anything."

The sentence hung in the air.

"If regular-sized people wound up in Cassoulet Reserve, it stands to reason that there might be some here," said Juliet.

Damian nodded yes as he walked slowly through the underbrush. "It's like we're starting fresh. I don't know where anything is? I don't know where to go or what to do."

"It's so quiet," said Juliet. "The helicopter made a lot of noise when they dropped us off. I wonder where the giants are."

"I'm sorry I got you involved in this, luv," he said.

"Don't be silly. I went along willingly. I mean, you were going to get me out of the reserve and you did."

"Only to get you back in another one."

Juliet took in the comment, then said, "How could you have known that would happen."

"What's that noise?" said Damian.

"I don't hear anything."

He stopped. "Movement. Something's coming towards us." Damian strained his eyes and saw several figures through the trees in the distance.

"Do you see that?" he asked.

"No. What?" Juliet remembered that giants have superior vision. "I don't have your super eye sight."

"Something is moving toward us." He paused for several seconds. "Something big."

Juliet perched herself on Damian's shoulder, strained her eyes again and could barely make out whatever was coming.

"What did you mean when you said 'something big?'"

"Big like me."

"It looks like a man," she said. She kept looking.

"No," said Damian. "It's a woman. A bunch of women." He strained his eyes again. "But..."

"But what?"

"They're all giants."

Juliet took in the information, but was having a hard time processing it. She squinted again. This time she could see clearer.

"You're right," she said. As she watched, she could see that they were indeed women walking briskly towards them.

Damian stopped and waited. Within seconds, he was staring at the faces of three female giants, all about his size. Juliet gauged them to be in their late teens-to-early twenties. Unlike the giants in Cassoulet Reserve, these women were attractive. They stared at Damian, looking at him curiously, but saying nothing.

Damian and Juliet stared back silently.

Finally, Juliet shouted, "We are from America. We speak English. Do you speak English?"

Silence for what seemed like an eternity, then a male voice said, "*I* do. I mean, we all do."

He was on the right shoulder of one of the giant women. He was a teenaged boy, who looked to be sixteen or seventeen years old with shoulder-length, brown hair. He tapped the shoulder of the giant he was on and said, "Let me down, Liana." She lowered him to the ground gently.

"We heard your call," he said, then he moved closer to Juliet, totally disinterested in Damian. "We were close by."

Juliet's and Damian's eyes were still transfixed on the huge women before them.

Ignoring Damian, the teenaged boy walked directly to Juliet. He had a tremendous smile on his face.

"My name is Jannik," he said excitedly. He focused his attention on Juliet. "You are from America. That is so cool. What is your name?" Juliet detected a slight Italian accent.

"Juliet."

"Like from *Romeo and Juliet*?" he asked.

"No. I was named after my grandmother."

"And you speak English?" said Jannik.

"Yes. How did you get in this place?"

He rolled his blue eyes. "Plane crash."

"Me too."

"Almost eight years ago, when I was nine years old, both of my parents were killed. The giants saved me. They raised me." Jannik looked confused. "I don't understand. Your plane crashed *here*?"

"No. In America. Where we're from."

He looked even more baffled. "How did you get here?"

"It's a long story," she said.

"I'm so happy to see you, Juliet. You have to tell me everything that's gone on in the world for the last eight years."

Before she could answer, three more female giants appeared from beyond the trees. One of them, with long red hair, caught Damian's attention. He couldn't take his eyes off of her.

"Who's the girl with the red hair?" asked Damian as he stared at the young giant girl he guessed was about fifteen.

"Her name is Melisar," said Jannik.

Damian kept staring at Melisar, specifically at her fiery red hair. He had never seen hair that color before. Like him, she was perfectly symmetrical to her size.

Juliet watched as Damian took in the beautiful female giant. She smiled.

Damian smiled at Melisar and said, "I'm Damian."

He wasn't sure why, but he extended his right hand.

She smiled at him and said, "Hello." She clasped Damian's hand, then stared at his ring for several seconds, then she pulled her hand away and looked not so much frightened, but awestruck.

"What's wrong, Melisar?" asked Jerrik.

"He's wearing the ring," she said. "The ring of Chambéry."

All the giants froze. Linea moved close to Damian, bent over, took his hand and gazed at the ring.

"I didn't believe you would come," said Linea, continuing to study the ring.

"What's going on?" said Damian.

"Your mother's prediction is true," said Juliet excitedly. "She said you would be a leader. The only thing she got wrong was the place."

Damian heard something in the distance. Movement. "Something's coming towards us."

Suddenly, all the female giants looked concerned.

"Is it the gigantem?" asked Jerrik.

"Yes," said Liana.

What's the gigantem?

"We have to get out of here," said Jerrik

"What is the gigantem?" asked Juliet. "And why do we have to get out of here?"

"They're our enemy," said Jerrik. "We need to leave. Come with us." He turned to the giant who was carrying him. "Linea. Up."

She bent down, lowered her hand and lifted Jerrik. "Follow us," he said. "To the caves." He pointed to his left. "Over there."

"Wait," said Damian. "Why can't I meet these other giants?"

"There's no time now," said Jerrik. "I'll explain later. Follow us."

Melisar glanced at Damian, then turned and joined the other giants as they ran off.

"Damian, what should we do?" asked Juliet, panicked.

Damian strained his eyes and saw several figures through the trees in the distance.

"More giants are coming and they're bigger than me." He strained his eyes again. "I mean, six or seven feet taller. Maybe even more."

Juliet took in the information, but was having a hard time processing it.

They're taller than Damian?

She squinted again. This time she could see more clearly.

"They look like they're twenty-five feet high."

"More like thirty. And they're all fat and ugly. They look like Hughie and Victor."

"And they look angry," said Juliet.

Damian stopped and waited. Within seconds, he was staring up at the hideous faces of seven giants. Each one was more frightening-looking then the next. Juliet guessed them to be in their early-to-mid-twenties. They stared down at Damian, breathing heavily, unshaven, some were drooling, others were scratching themselves, a few had limbs missing, two were mumbling like crazy people, but they all were looking at him curiously, but saying nothing as they surrounded them.

Damian and Juliet stared back silently.

Finally, Juliet shouted, "We are from America. We speak English. Do you speak English?"

Silence for what seemed like an eternity, then one of the giants shouted in a gravely grunt, "Get him!"

Three of the giants rushed to Damian and tried to grab him, but because they were so big, they were having a hard time holding on to him. They managed to knock him over, which sent Juliet spiraling to the ground. Somehow Damian was able to catch her before she landed. He set her on the grass.

Because it was happening so fast, Juliet was caught off guard for several seconds, then she screamed, "We don't want any trouble. We want to be your friends."

Was that a dumb thing to say?

One of the giants not holding Damian waved his right hand and knocked her sideways, sending her about fifteen feet away, stunning her.

Witnessing this, Damian became enraged. He kicked one of the giants in the kneecap knocking him over, punched another one in the solar plexus, bit the hand of another and got free, then he ran to Juliet.

"You okay, luv?"

"Yes. What are we gonna do?"

"We have to get away from them." Damian was about to pick her up, when he was upended when one of the giants grabbed his feet.

"Damian!" screamed Juliet.

A second giant came to the aid of the one holding on to Damian's feet. With both of them having a firm grip, Damian couldn't do anything. They started pulling him away.

"Damian!"

"Run!" Damian screamed. "Juliet, run."

Juliet hesitated for a few seconds.

"Where?" she shouted.

"To the caves," screamed Damian. "I'll find you, luv!" She stared at him, helplessly.

And then he was dragged away.

With Damian's warning echoing in her ears, she turned and started running as fast as she could in the direction that Jerrik ran with the female giants. She didn't stop to look back. She kept pushing herself until she couldn't breathe, then she stopped and turned around to see if a giant was following her.

She couldn't see anything except trees, endless disorganized rows of trees. And there was silence. Total silence. She felt fragile, like a helpless child. She pressed on, walking slowly now, towards the caves. She would locate Jerrik and ask him to help her do two things: find Damian and then escape from the White Forest.

Night was falling, and the skies were darkening. She was terrified of being alone.

Then she heard a hideous howling in the distance she was heading toward. It was a combination growl and a scream. It was unhuman. She heard it again. And again. It petrified her.

She remembered the line from *Game of Thrones*.

The night is dark and full of terrors.

The growling stopped, and it was quiet again.

I have to keep going. I have to.

She took a deep breath and kept on walking.

The End

To Be Continued
In
Book 2
The White Forest Monster